'I don't believe we've been introduced,' Leon said. 'Want to shake hands?' And, not a bit abashed by his own nakedness, he looked as if he was about to get out of bed...

The man was no stranger to Varnie, not since she had seen that picture of him in the paper yesterday. There was absolutely no need for the man to introduce himself. She already knew who he was.

But what in blazes was Leon Beaumont doing here? And, more worrying than that, he—the first man ever to do so—had just seen her completely stark naked, stitchless. Oh, heavens above, how on earth was she ever to face him again?

Jessica Steele lives in a friendly Worcestershire village with her super husband, Peter. They are owned by a gorgeous Staffordshire bull terrier called Florence, who is boisterous and manic, but also adorable. It was Peter who first prompted Jessica to try writing, and, after the first rejection, encouraged her to keep on trying. Luckily, with the exception of Uruguay, she has so far managed to research inside all the countries in which she has set her books, travelling to places as far apart as Siberia and Egypt. Her thanks go to Peter for his help and encouragement.

Recent titles by the same author:

HER BOSS'S MARRIAGE AGENDA
A PAPER MARRIAGE
AN ACCIDENTAL ENGAGEMENT
A PROFESSIONAL MARRIAGE
HIS PRETEND MISTRESS

A PRETEND ENGAGEMENT

BY
JESSICA STEELE

MILLS & BOON®

MILLS & BOON and MILLS & BOON with the Rose Device are registered trademarks of the publisher.

First published in Great Britain 2004
Harlequin Mills & Boon Limited,
Eton House, 18-24 Paradise Road, Richmond, Surrey TW9 1SR

© Jessica Steele 2004

ISBN 0 263 83842 0

Set in Times Roman 10½ on 11¼ pt.
02-0804-56492

Printed and bound in Spain
by Litografía Rosés, S.A., Barcelona

CHAPTER ONE

HER thoughts were many and varied during that long drive from Heathrow airport to North Wales. Nor were her thoughts the happiest. It did not cheer her one whit that fog had descended, making it a truly murky, damp and miserable November night. The night matched her mood.

She had hoped to make the journey to Aldwyn House in Denbighshire in record time, but poor visibility made any chance of driving at speed out of the question. To speed in these conditions would be utter madness.

Not that she had intended to drive to Wales when she had first left the airport. Her initial thought, an unconscious thought, had been to drive back to her home near Cheltenham. An hour into the drive, however, and Varnie had recalled all the stresses and strains her overworked parents had endured recently. The last thing she wanted to do, now that they were retired and sailing in calmer waters, was to give them cause to be upset or anxious again—especially about her.

They'd had more than enough to worry about, first with her brother, Johnny, crashing his car—though it was true he always seemed to be about an inch away from some disaster or other—and then her father being diagnosed with high blood pressure. Johnny had walked away from his car crash with barely a scratch, but they had all worried about him. On top of that the hotel they owned had started to lose money, and they had decided to try and sell it. And then Grandfather Sutton had died. One way and another it had been a pretty anxious time.

But, looking on the brighter side, the hotel had at last sold and, wonder of wonders, Johnny, at twenty-five—and something of a misfit—had at last found his niche, and was finally settled in a job he absolutely loved. So, all in all, their parents should now be able to look forward to the stress-free life that they so thoroughly deserved.

No way, Varnie had realised, could she go back home to lick her wounds. With the best acting in the world she knew she had no hope of hiding how very let down and upset she was feeling. And, on fretting about it, Varnie had just known that she had no need to go home; her parents were not expecting to see her again for two weeks anyway!

Varnie had changed course and felt distinctly out of sorts as she'd dwelt on how only that morning her parents had stood on the drive of their new home and waved her a smiling goodbye. She had been smiling too, experiencing quite a flutter of happy anticipation at the prospect of sharing a whole two weeks in Switzerland with her boyfriend Martin.

Because he worked so hard, holidays were a rarity for Martin. He was only able to take this trip now because he was able to combine it with some business. But when he was not engaged in business they would be together, and it would be a chance for them to really get to know each other—so she had thought.

Varnie was not smiling now. In fact she was feeling far from happy as she headed for Wales. By sheer good fortune she had popped her keys to Aldwyn House into the glove compartment of her car on her last visit there.

Oh, what a fool she had been! What a total and complete idiot! How could she…? My heavens, if she had not started to grow a bit fidgety when Martin Walker had been three-quarters of an hour adrift from the time they had arranged to meet at the airport, she would even now be on some plane with him about to land in Switzerland!

It was only because he was meant to be partly on holiday that she had broken his 'Don't-ring-me-at-the-office. We're-so-busy-and-I'm-always-dashing-all-over-the-place, and-they'll-never-find-me' rule. But she had tried ringing his mobile—it was switched off.

She had fidgeted some more. Walked around a little—with luggage. And eventually, with the view of trying not to keep a fixed gaze on the entrances into the departures area, she had gone and purchased a newspaper. On opening the paper, however, her mind for a very brief while had been taken away from Martin Walker. Because there on the very front page was a picture of one man felling some other man—with a headline telling her that the man doing the felling was none other than her brother's new boss, Leon Beaumont. The photographer had caught him just after he had thrown his punch and as the other man hit the ground. Good heavens!

Swiftly she'd read what it was all about. Apparently, and 'allegedly', in newspaper speak, which meant there was probably very little doubt about it, Leon Beaumont had been making out with one of his female executives—there was a picture to the side of one very elegant and attractive thirty or so brunette, name Antonia King—and her husband had got to hear of the liaison.

Why Neville King was the one on the floor, a hand going to his recently thumped jaw, and not the other way round, was not stated. But Leon Beaumont looked angry enough to give him more of the same once the cuckolded husband managed to get to his feet.

Varnie had lost interest. She didn't think much of men who went around knocking other men to the ground—even if this particular pugilist was the employer her brother admired so much. Oh, where was Martin? If he didn't soon arrive…

She had checked her watch for the umpteenth time, and had known that if she were going to make that call to his office that she had better do it now. The firm's switchboard would be closing in ten minutes. She had given it another three, and still no Martin.

She'd had enough. He was supposed to be on holiday, for goodness' sake. She'd taken out her phone—she would make just the one call, then she would switch her phone off too, ready for the flight.

Glad she had thought to take a note of Martin's number, a number she had never before called, Varnie had pressed out the digits. Martin had a new secretary; she hoped she wasn't the sort who took off ten minutes early on a Friday night.

She wasn't. The telephonist had soon put her through.

'Oh, hello,' Varnie said brightly, conjuring up the female's name from somewhere, 'Is that Becky?'

'That's me,' answered a sweet girlish voice.

'Martin isn't there by any chance, is he?'

'Oh, no. He left ages ago!' Becky replied, much to Varnie's relief. But before she could thank her, say goodbye and switch off her phone, Becky was enthusiastically enquiring, 'You and the children got to Kenilworth all right, then, Mrs Walker?'

'I'm not…' Mrs Walker! His mother? Children? 'Mrs Walker?' Varnie enquired evenly—five years in the hotel trade had taught her to mask any slight feeling of inner foreboding, even though she knew she had not the smallest need to feel in any way disquieted.

'I'm sorry,' Becky apologised at once. 'You're not Mrs Walker, are you?' and, going on without pause, she excused, 'Only, Mrs Walker—Melanie—and the children were in here just after lunch. She and the little ones were just going off to stay with her mother while her husband's away on business.'

Feeling shaken to the roots of her being, Varnie was speechless—and disbelieving! Her brain wasn't taking in what it very much sounded as if Becky was trying to impart. 'Er—Martin is married to Melanie?' she managed when, knowing she must have misunderstood, she got her breath back.

But, 'That's right,' Becky answered cheerfully. 'Such a happy couple together. Martin hated having to leave her, but business is business and—'

Varnie abruptly ended the call. Without another word she switched off her phone and sat totally stunned. There was some mistake! There must be. For heaven's sake, Martin had told her he loved her and that this trip, this two weeks, would be a time of them getting really close. She had been excited at the idea. Martin was always so busy that the only times they had been able to see each other had been when he'd been Cheltenham way on business and had stayed overnight at her parents' hotel.

Why, her parents had liked him! Had wished her well when she had explained that this trip was about her and Martin making up for all those weekends when he had been too busy to see her. Her parents knew all about busy weekends. The hotel business was a seven-days-a-week business.

But doubt, small at first, suddenly started to creep in. Varnie pulled her suitcase nearer to her and tried to think of one single, solitary weekend that she'd had free at the same time as Martin. She could not think of one!

The significance of that, when partnered up with his secretary Becky's remarks just now, started to creep in. Was Martin busy every weekend—or was it that he had to spend his weekends with his wife and children? Children!

Unable to take such thoughts sitting down, Varnie got abruptly to her feet. 'Martin is married…?' she had asked. 'That's right. Such a happy couple together.' And don't forget 'the little ones'. And do *not* forget 'Martin hated having to leave her'. Her—his wife!

Varnie had moved two steps when she saw Martin, a huge grin on his face when he saw her, come dashing in. 'I'm so sorry, my sweet darling,' he apologised, simply oozing charm. 'The traffic was a—' He broke off when he saw that Varnie was looking more frosty than loving. 'What—?'

'Tell me straight,' Varnie cut in. 'Are you married?'

'I—um…' He started to bluster, and Varnie went cold. She had somehow fully expected a swift and outright denial. 'Hey—what's this?' he asked, recovering, his boyish grin blasting out as he attempted to take a familiar hold of her arm.

'Are you?' Varnie insisted, while at the same time hating herself that, had he said no, she would still probably have believed him. 'Are you?' she repeated firmly.

'Well—um… We're separated.' He quickly got himself together. 'We're going to divorce. I haven't seen her in ages, but I'm planning to get my solicitor to contact hers the minute you and I get back to…'

Varnie went from merely being cold to icy. She stooped to pick up her suitcase. 'Goodbye, Martin,' she said, and guessed that her expression must have told him that anything else he had to say could be said to the air, that she was not interested in him or his lies, because he did not try to stop her from leaving.

Nor *was* she interested in anything else he had to say. She felt wretched. She felt sick. And she was having the hardest time in accepting just how easily she had been duped. How easily her parents, too, who were far more worldly-wise than she, had also been so taken in by Martin Walker's smooth charm.

Varnie went in search of her car with her mind in a turmoil.

He was married! Martin Walker was a married man and—all too plainly—still living with his wife! He—they—had children! And her—he had been dating her!

True, their dates had been more kind of snatched moments when he was in the Cheltenham area. But—she had been going to go away with him, for goodness' sake.

She felt frozen up inside and bitterly betrayed. He had fooled her, and he had fooled her parents.

Her thoughts started to wander and she went back to when they had first met Martin. He had stayed overnight at their smart but modestly priced hotel. She had served him drinks in the bar and they had got talking. He was thirty-four, he had openly told her, and was working all hours trying to make a go of his own business. She had relayed that to her parents. They had approved. Hadn't they done the same? Were they still not doing the same? And until the hotel, then recently put on the market, found a buyer, they would go on doing the same.

Purchasers for small independent hotels were not that thick on the ground, and they had all still been beavering away three months later—with Martin Walker now a frequent overnight guest. He'd begun to take an interest in Varnie. She'd liked him. Her parents had smiled on when occasionally he would spend two consecutive nights at their hotel; they'd more or less left her to deal with him.

Somehow she and Martin had become a couple. He would phone her daily, usually around three in the afternoon, when she was in the office typing up menus or doing some book-keeping. Varnie made a point of being in the office at that time, though she was used to 'filling in' whenever some member of staff rang to say they had child-minding problems, toothache, or whatever misadventure had befallen them so they could not work their shift.

But because both she and Martin were fully stretched work-wise—he getting his business off the ground and she as well as working what were termed 'unsocial hours' taking on extra duties—their warming friendship had seemed to stay just that.

Then Mrs Lloyd, the woman who'd cooked and cleaned for Grandfather Sutton at Aldwyn House, had rung to say she had found him collapsed on the drawing room floor and had called a doctor. Typically, he had refused to go to hospital, and Varnie and her mother had dashed to North Wales to see him.

Varnie swallowed hard as she recalled that dreadful time. Grandfather Sutton had died three days later, and she had so loved him. She had been his only blood relation, and he'd liked her to spend all her childhood holidays with him. Johnny would come too, often, and her grandfather would treat them both the same, albeit that Johnny was in actual fact his step-grandson—her stepbrother.

Johnny's father was the only father Varnie had known. She had been an infant when her own father had died, and two years old—Johnny five—when his divorced father had married her mother. Varnie had kept the name Sutton, but felt fully a member of the Metcalfe family. Johnny's father loved her like the father she had never known.

Martin Walker had been there at the hotel when they had returned from Wales after her grandfather's funeral, Varnie recalled as she motored on. Johnny had loved Grandfather Sutton too, and had been with them. Varnie knew she had been feeling emotional and vulnerable, so that when Martin had taken her in his arms and had told her that he loved her she had rather thought that she loved him too. She abruptly blocked her mind off to that, what she now knew to be a false memory, and attempted to concentrate on something else. What? Johnny?

Johnny, her clever but butterfly-brained brother. He had wanted absolutely nothing at all to do with the hotel trade, and had made tracks for London as soon as he could. In actual fact he had a fine brain, and if he ever applied himself to go into business for himself—and stuck to it—it was a foregone conclusion he would make a success of it. But for all his bright brain, or maybe because of it, he was easily bored and never seemed to stay long with any one firm. Needing money, however, he would work for it. His last few jobs had seen him deskbound—until boredom had set in.

'I've been made redundant,' he'd said cheerfully, when his previous job had ended abruptly.

'Oh, Johnny, I'm so sorry,' she had sympathised.

'I'm not.' He had laughed. 'Now what?'

Oh, Johnny, Johnny. Varnie thought fondly. The fog was seeming to become thicker than ever, making driving conditions even more hazardous. It seemed she and her parents had spent most of their lives worrying about Johnny. He seemed to have the most uncanny knack of getting into twice as many scrapes as other men his age. How well she remembered the time he had written his car off, and how they had charged up to London, terrified of what he might have done to himself—only to find that he had discharged himself from hospital and gone for a pint at his local. Sometimes they were certain that Johnny must come from some other planet.

Then, with the exception of her grandfather passing away, things had started to look up. The hotel had sold and their parents had purchased a new home, and, with money over, Johnny had been promised a lump sum when all finances were settled. Johnny had immediately made arrangements to go to Australia to spend a month with friends he had there.

Shortly afterwards, and to put the icing on his particular cake, he had found the job he said he had been looking for all his working life. 'It's the job of my dreams, Varnie!' he'd enthused, and she'd thought she would have to tie him to a chair if he got any more excited.

The job was as peripatetic assistant to one Leon Beaumont. Apparently the great man was often out of the office, either travelling around Britain or abroad. But so keen, not to say desperate, had Johnny been to get the job, he had been ready to cancel his proposed Australian holiday. It had not come to that, because, having been offered the job, he'd found that Leon Beaumont was prepared to honour his holiday arrangements. As it happened those arrangements conveniently fitted in with a break he was thinking of taking himself.

In actual fact Johnny's Australia-bound flight had taken off earlier that day, Varnie reflected. But, not wanting to think about airports, she recalled how her father—stepfather, to be absolutely accurate—had wanted to give her a lump sum too. But by then she had learned that Grandfather Sutton had left Aldwyn House to her. And, though she knew she would not be able to afford the upkeep of the big old house, and would, reluctantly, have to sell it, she also realised that she would make a considerable amount from the sale, and did not therefore feel able to accept her father's generous offer.

She had little money of her own, but was heartily glad she had paid her own airfare to Switzerland. Though it would have served Martin Walker right if she *had* allowed him to pay for it—but in all probability he would have been able to cash her ticket in. Come to think of it, she could not recall him ever offering to pay her fare.

It had been a very big step for her to have agreed to go with him in the first place. It wasn't as if she had ever done that sort of thing before. But, what with all the upheaval that had happened, the trauma of losing Grandfather, she had been rather looking forward to a break herself. And, she reminded herself, don't forget she had loved Martin.

Had? That word brought her up short as, the foggy conditions not improving the least bit, she drove carefully on. *Had* she loved Martin? Grief, she must have done! Hadn't she been thinking of getting herself some kind of a career in London so that she should be nearer to him, so that they might see more of each other?

Yet what did she feel now? Anger, mainly. Fury that there were such ghastly men about. She felt duped, soiled, and it was none of her making. She felt a sort of numbness too, and wondered if that numbness was perhaps a precursor to the pain she was bound to feel when that numbness wore off.

She knew then that she had made the right decision not to go home. She did not feel up to facing her parents' concern for her, nor did she want them to be concerned. They'd had enough of an anxious time. Perhaps she could spend the two weeks she was supposed to be in Switzerland in getting herself together at her grandfather's home. His death was so recent she still thought of Aldwyn House as her grandfather's home.

Varnie wanted her parents to have some quiet time with each other. Oh, how they had earned it. A time together with no hotel to worry them, a time of tranquility, with their children off on their own happy pursuits and without traumas various happening in their worlds.

Varnie became aware that her eyes were feeling dreadfully gritty from her efforts of concentrating so hard on her driving in such diabolical conditions. At the very next opportunity she pulled off the motorway—to discover, when she went to search out a cup of coffee, that everyone else had the same idea.

When she was eventually served she found a spare seat at a table and decided to stay where she was for a while. She did not fancy at all driving the tortuous mountain roads if this fog were a blanket over the whole country.

But eventually, aware that other people were coming in all the while, she vacated her place and went to sit in her car. She was glad then to feel angry again that through no fault of her own—expect perhaps blind trusting gullibility— she was where she was anyway, and not safely tucked up in her own bed at home.

Men! she fumed, though had to modify that when she thought of the sweetness that had been her grandfather, the loving generosity that was the man her mother had married—Johnny's father—and Johnny himself, given that Johnny had always seemed to be getting himself into some sort of scrape or another. They were always honest scrapes, though. Well, she had to qualify, honest since he had left his boyhood behind. Which honesty was more than could be said for Martin Walker. How honest was it to tell one woman you loved her while married and still living with another? He even had children that she had known nothing about! Men! She'd had it with the lot of them.

Why—look at Leon Beaumont! She had evidence for her own eyes in the paper today of what an adulterous swine he was. Varnie searched the recesses of her mind for information she would probably have given no heed to if her brother had not gone to work for him. Hadn't Leon Beaumont been involved in some divorce scandal only recently? Hadn't he been toting around some other married lovely, whose marriage had ended in divorce on account of him?

Somehow she found that she could not get thoughts of Leon Beaumont out of her head. Which was odd, because until she had seen that picture of him today, having just thumped Neville King and waiting for him to get up so he could give him another one, she'd had no idea of what the man her brother admired so much looked like.

He was tall, that much was obvious, even when bent over from decking the man on the floor. Good-looking too— dark-haired, athletic-looking—and loaded. As Johnny had said, as bachelors went, they didn't come any more eligible. Varnie was unimpressed—she was off mid-thirties men, and Leon Beaumont looked only a year or two older than Martin Walker.

But where Martin was trying to build up a business—if what he said was true—Leon Beaumont, head of an international design and development company in the field of communication systems, had already done that.

That was according to Johnny who, while waiting to know if he had got the job as Leon Beaumont's assistant, had never ceased singing the man's praises.

Apparently the man already had a PA who was little short of brilliant. So brilliant, in fact, that when she'd married last year, and then started to fret about being apart from her new husband when called to go on the many trips out of London and out of the country, Leon had taken action. Rather than lose his gem of a PA, he'd decided she could stay office-bound and he would create the new position of peripatetic assistant, who, when they were both in the office, could give her a hand.

Johnny was well versed in office routine, a wizard with his laptop and anything to do with computers. Plus, he had a pleasing personality and having learned something of a lesson from his car crash, was a very good driver.

To start with he had truly believed the position advertised would go to some female, but he'd felt he had interviewed well. There had then followed a period of him phoning home every day in panic that he had heard nothing, and they'd been in no doubt, as the days had gone by, that he would feel totally crushed if he did not get the job.

'I'd work the first three months for nothing if only he'd give me the chance,' Varnie remembered him saying one time. That, she realised, from a brother who never seemed to have any spare cash, just proved how desperate he had been to have the job.

The day he'd rung to say he had actually been offered the job, actually had the letter in his hand, Varnie had been so glad for him. Though she had thought that some of his enthusiasm might wane when he had been in the job for a month.

But, no, not a bit of it. Leon Beaumont could do no wrong, it seemed. Johnny drove him all over the country—and learned a great deal by just watching the man in action. Leon was this, Leon was that, and, though he did not suffer fools gladly, Johnny had never met a more fair-minded man. He took neither nonsense nor favours from anyone. In business he was his own man, and would not be indebted to anyone.

Johnny had driven him to one of their plants—the technology was absolutely amazing. He had been enthralled, and had subsequently taken notes at some high-powered meeting and, having prior to his interview taken an emergency course in speedwriting, been little short of ecstatic that he had got it all typed back perfectly and accurately.

Given that Johnny had a harum-scarum tendency, they had always known he had a fine brain—when he cared to exercise it. But, in short, having so desperately wanted this job, having got it, he was so happy, and was determined to do everything to keep it and to make his employer think well of him.

Which, she decided, with the hotel sold, Johnny settled and her parents settled, made her the only odd one out. Her parents thought that everything would now be fine and that they could sit back and relax—so how could she go home now and ruffle the calmer waters of their life?

Feeling glad she had made the decision she had, to drive by Cheltenham and head for the Welsh mountains, Varnie knew even so that she would not be sorry to reach Aldwyn House and her bed.

The moment she hit those twisting mountain roads though, she had little space to think of anything but where she was heading. She felt as though she had been driving for a dozen or so hours, and it was in fact after midnight when she at last hit a straightish run of road where she had space to once again let her thoughts in. But oddly, while her family and Martin Walker had their fair share in her thoughts, it seemed as though Leon Beaumont, a man she had never met, was determined to have an equal part in her head.

'Oh, clear off,' she actually muttered aloud, when the picture she'd seen of Leon Beaumont in the paper jumped into her mind's eye. He might be scrupulously fair in his business life, but it was a pity he didn't run his personal life so scrupulously!

It was one in the morning by the time she passed the little clutch of cottages that were the nearest neighbours to Aldwyn House. A quarter of a mile further on and Varnie climbed stiffly from her car to open the gates to the property.

She drove through, but felt too weary suddenly to bother to close them behind her.

'Have a wonderful holiday,' her parents had bidden her. Varnie had not visualised then that she would be spending the next two weeks not skiing, but here at Aldwyn House.

She left her car standing in front of the garage. All at once she felt too used up to try and do battle with the heavy garage doors—she would put her car away in the morning. Similarly, the front door sometimes stuck in the damp winter months. She was too tired to contemplate finding the energy to wrestle with it.

With her house keys and flight bag in one hand, her suitcase in the other, and with some vague notion to take a shower prior to falling straight into bed, Varnie went to the rear of the house and let herself in through the kitchen door.

She noticed at once as she snicked on the light that someone had been there. She didn't mind. Johnny had a key. He was a kind soul, and while she and their parents had been dealing with packing that which the new owners of the hotel were not taking over he had volunteered to come and empty her grandfather's wardrobes and drawers.

Switching lights on and off as she went, Varnie left the kitchen, having noted that while Johnny had not got around to putting away the cup and saucer he must have used when he'd made himself some black coffee, he had rinsed them and left them drying on the draining board. She went up the stairs and to the room she always used when she visited. It was a pretty room, with a lovely view, and though not as large as the master bedroom it was a room she preferred.

Seated on the side of the bed, she eased off her shoes and reflected on one of the worst days of her life. But, bed calling, she got up, glad she had left the bed made up from her last visit. But when she went to unlock her suitcase she suddenly felt too weary to remember in which of the many compartments of her flight bag she had put the key.

'Oh, hang it,' she mumbled, and stripped off. Deciding

for once not to obey the habit of a lifetime and shower before bed, she climbed into bed—and went out like the proverbial light.

As weary as she had been, however, she was awake at her usual time of six o'clock. She lay there in the pitch darkness and was briefly surprised that after all that had happened yesterday she had slept at all.

Then all at once several things struck her that she had been too weary when she had arrived to pay any heed to. The house was warm! Johnny again. The house was built of stone, almost two feet thick in places, which made it lovely during a heatwave, but bitterly cold in winter. Johnny must have put the central heating on when he'd arrived and forgotten to turn if off again when he left. Thank you, Johnny.

She clicked on the bedside lamp, smiling fondly as she thought of him. She hoped he had a fantastic holiday in Australia. His friends Danny and Diana Haywood would make him more than welcome, she knew that.

But, in the meantime, she would not have to make do with the low-powered hit and miss, not to say downright temperamental shower in her adjoining bathroom. She could use the brilliant and powerful one in the bathroom adjoining the master bedroom.

Varnie toyed with the notion of shaking some clothes out from her suitcase first, but all at once to take the shower she had missed last night seemed to be something of a priority.

Modesty was simply not required, and, stark naked, she left her room and padded along the landing to grab a large towel from the big airing cupboard as she went. She had the house all to herself after all. Not a soul there to see her.

With a towel over one arm, she trundled along to the master bedroom and opened the door. Her mind more on crossing the room to the door of the bathroom than anything, Varnie flicked on the light switch and was halfway across the room when all of a sudden it was borne startlingly in on her that she was very far from alone!

She wasn't even looking at the bed when her peripheral vision detected the movement of bedcovers! She stared, stunned, at the bed. But before her brain could leap into action, electric light flooding the room had alerted the other occupant to another presence, and a body began to emerge!

'What the...?' His sleep disturbed by the sudden glare of light, the man was not thrilled and was already sitting up. And, by the look of his naked chest and hip as the bedcovers started to go back, he was as stark naked as she!

'H...? Wh...? Oh!' she gasped, frozen to the spot, her brain totally seized up as she stared, her sea-green eyes saucer-wide, at the dark-haired man about to leave the bed.

Her shaken rigid expression, her scarlet face, must have got through to the man. However, she was sure it was not to spare her blushes that he halted briefly and remarked, a shade toughly, she felt, 'I don't believe we've been introduced,' adding, much in the same tone, 'Want to shake hands?'

And, not a bit abashed by his own nakedness, he looked about to get out of bed—though not before he took a slow inventory of her—assets. His eyes—grey, she noticed, quite ridiculously, she afterwards felt—travelled meticulously from the top of her tousled long blonde hair, down over her face and, resting perhaps a fraction longer than necessary over her pink-tipped breasts, down over her belly and slender hips, past her beautifully shaped long, long legs.

But by the time he reached her toes Varnie was released from the shock that had kept her frozen still and was suddenly galvanised into action. Without a word or another glance at him, as one of his legs came from beneath the covers and it seemed he was going to stand up and shake hands anyway, Varnie got out of there. Had she had space, time, and had her head not been alive with horror she would have attempted to cover her fleeing naked buttocks with the towel, but she was much more concerned with doing a quick disappearing act.

She reached her room and slammed the door hard shut, to find she was breathing hard and shaking from head to foot. Johnny! Johnny Metcalfe, her brother—stepbrother, if you must. She'd stepbrother him! If he wasn't in Australia, if she could get her hands on her, she'd kill him.

How could he? And it had to be him! He had invited a perfect stranger to sleep overnight at what was now, she started to accept, her place.

Johnny knew who he was, of course. The man was no stranger to him. And not totally a stranger to her either, not since she had seen that picture of him in the paper yesterday. There was absolutely no need for the man to introduce himself. She already knew who he was.

But what in blazes was Leon Beaumont doing here? And, more worrying than that, he—the first man ever to do so— had just seen her completely stark naked—stitchless. Oh, heavens above, how on earth was she ever to face him again?

CHAPTER TWO

HASTILY, flicking nervous glances to her slammed shut bedroom door from time to time, just in case Leon Beaumont should take it into his head to follow her, Varnie wrapped the large towel around her shape and searched her flight bag for the key to her case. With fumbling, agitated fingers she unlocked her case and extracted underwear, trousers and a shirt.

She heard plumbing noises and hated Leon Beaumont that he, when she was too panic-stricken to think of taking a shower in case he walked in, as nice as you please, was showering, quite unconcerned.

Varnie broke another unwritten rule. She rinsed her face and then dressed without first showering. After running a comb through her hair she left her room, went down the stairs and went into the kitchen—to wait.

He was in no particular hurry, it seemed, and still hadn't appeared five minutes later. But, while still not looking forward to seeing him again—she went red just thinking of how she had stood, positively starkers, in front of him—she was beginning to feel much calmer than she had.

The longer he kept her waiting, though, and she was starting to think that perhaps there was no need for her to face the embarrassment of seeing him again. Johnny would have told him that his sister owned the house and... Or would he? There was no knowing with Johnny. At times that clever brother of hers could be totally feather-brained. It could be, she realised, that Leon Beaumont had not the smallest clue who she was. So why didn't she just open that door, take a fast walk to her car, and get out of there? She could be back home in Gloucestershire by...

Hang on a minute, this was *her* house! Not his! And anyway, she wasn't ready to go home yet. Soon the pain of Martin Walker's perfidiousness would start, and she would prefer to be alone here rather than at home with her parents when that happened. She wanted to leave them in peace, blissfully believing she was abroad enjoying the ski slopes.

And on the thought that she had come here to be alone Varnie decided that it was time she got her act together. Time she took charge of the situation. She had no idea what Leon Beaumont was doing here, but she wasn't leaving— he was!

Feeling in a sudden determined frame of mind, Varnie marched from the kitchen and along the hall to the bottom of the stairs. There she listened for sounds of the electric motor that would tell her that Beaumont was making the most of his shower. She could hear nothing, so knew he was out of the shower.

Preferring not to see him in any stage of undress, she decided against going up the stairs to give him his marching orders. He might be her brother's boss, but he wasn't hers. She was about to go back to the kitchen when she spotted a whole pile of junk mail on the floor by the front door. There was masses of it, and since she had cleared away anything that had come through the letter flap on her last visit…

Thinking to occupy herself while waiting for his lordship—what on earth had Johnny been thinking to give him his key?—she went and collected up the mound of clear plastic covered unsolicited mail. Then she found that one was a plain white envelope.

Taking the mail with her back to the kitchen, she knew that the only explanation for Beaumont being inside her property must be because Johnny had handed over his key. Now, why would he do that?

She had a sudden flashback of standing with not a stitch on in front of the man her brother thought so highly of, and knew she was red about the ears. She swiftly busied herself opening up the unaddressed white envelope—and very quickly learned why, or part of why, her brother had parted with his key.

The letter was from Mrs Lloyd, the lady who had come to clean and cook for Grandfather Sutton, and was in response to a telephone call that Johnny had made to her. For all his name was not on the envelope, it began, 'Dear Mr Metcalfe'.

I am sorry I wasn't in when you rang yesterday. And I am sorry too that I am not able to come and look after your guest.

Apparently Mrs Lloyd was now retired but, if Mr Metcalfe was really stuck for someone, she had written the phone number of a Mrs Roberts who might be willing, if he could call daily and collect Mrs Roberts, who had no transport.

Her breath caught as it hit Varnie that this was not intended to be just a one-night stopover, as she'd thought! So, she fumed, cross with Johnny and fuming against his employer, that was it. Leon Beaumont obviously fancied a bit of a break—away from outraged husbands, no doubt—and Johnny, doubtless mentioning Aldwyn House, had decided it would be an ideal spot for a hideaway. And, without doubt too, would not have needed much coercion to hand over his key. Naturally enough Johnny, being Johnny and aware that she wouldn't be around for at least two weeks because she was flying off to Switzerland, had seen no need to inform her of what was happening. She felt fairly certain then that Johnny, as ever Johnny, just hadn't thought to tell his womanising employer that the property didn't actually belong to him.

The sound of footsteps interrupted her angry thoughts. She looked to the door. Leon Beaumont stood in the doorway. He was tall, as she had known he was. And, just as she had known she would, she went crimson.

He came further into the kitchen, but did not comment on her embarrassed colour; there wasn't so much as a hint of embarrassment about him, she noticed. But then, he was probably used to seeing the female form unclad, she fumed sniffily. Though before she could tell him that now that he was dressed she was throwing him out, he demanded, 'What's your name?'

As if it had anything to do with him! 'Varnie Sutton,' she answered snappily, and watched to see if her name meant anything to him. Clearly it didn't, so obviously Johnny had *not* thought to mention her. Not that he should in the ordinary run of things, but, dammit, this was her house! Realising that she was getting quite proprietorial about a house she would have to sell, Varnie decided it was high time she sent this man on his way. 'And you're Leon Beaumont,' she began stiffly. 'You—'

'You know who I am?' Beaumont demanded.

'Ever think you've wandered into someone else's nightmare?' she retorted.

He ignored that. 'How do you know who I am?' he barked curtly. 'Metcalfe had strict instructions that I wanted him to find me somewhere isolated where I wouldn't have to put up with—unwanted intrusions.'

Unwanted intrusions! By that did he mean he thought that she might come on to him? Varnie was on the instant up in arms. She was off men in general, and him in particular. 'For your information, I wouldn't touch you with a disinfected line-prop ten feet long!' she hissed. He favoured her with a searing look of scepticism. 'For your further information—' she went on.

'That's why you walked naked into my room, was it? Because you're not interested?' he cut in. 'Had I shown the smallest inclination you'd have been in that bed with me like a shot.'

Varnie stared at him in utter disbelief; the whole of her skin felt aflame. Somehow, though, she recovered, to tell him in no uncertain fashion, 'I'd sooner swallow prussic acid!' And, building up a fine head of steam, 'Your eyes were so busily engaged elsewhere…' She wished she hadn't said that. Her skin flamed anew as she again recalled his eyes going over her naked figure. '…otherwise you might have noticed I was carrying a towel. My only purpose in coming to that room was to take a shower. I didn't even know you were here.'

'What's wrong with the shower in your room?'

'My room?'

'I checked. You slept here last night.'

The cheeky swine! 'My shower needs fixing, there's hardly any pressure and the shower's better in your room.' Why was she bothering to explain? Good…

'You obviously know the house?'

'This isn't my first visit.'

Leon Beaumont stared at her, suspicion rife. 'From the size of your suitcase, you appear to have some notion of staying for a while?'

Did she have news for him. 'That's the general idea,' she replied. But before she could go on to tell him that she was staying and that he wasn't, he cut her short.

'You obviously know John Metcalfe.' Varnie was about to agree that she did, and that Johnny was her brother. But what Leon Beaumont said next brought her up very short, and caused her to hesitate. 'Obviously, too, you're also very well acquainted with my inefficient, new and soon to be short-lived assistant,' he rapped.

Varnie felt stumped. In an instant she recalled just how keen Johnny had been to work for this sharp and disgruntled-looking man. To work as Leon Beaumont's assistant, not deskbound but travelling all over—smoothing his path, so to speak, to leave him to deal with bigger, more important issues had been everything Johnny wanted! She gave an inner sigh—protecting Johnny, for all he was three years older than her, had over the years become second nature.

And that was when suddenly, albeit reluctantly, but without having to think about it, Varnie knew she was going to have to change her tune. If she did not, then by the look of it when Johnny came home from Australia, he would not have a job to come home to!

So, okay, she would stick up for Johnny, but no way was she going to crawl to this tall, dark-haired, grey-eyed man who had now come up close to her and was looking toughly, icily at her, through hard, cold and unfeeling grey eyes. 'Your assistant is extremely efficient,' she retorted.

'You know this?' he questioned, his hard gaze fixed on her sea-green eyes.

'I do,' she said, her mind racing to strive to think up something brilliant that Johnny had done.

'Surprise me?' Leon Beaumont's tone had turned to mockery.

'I—er—know for a fact that—that he tried to get some domestic help to cover while you're here,' she brought out triumphantly. Thank goodness she had read that letter.

'Mrs Lloyd?'

Rats! He already knew that. 'I arrived late last night,' Varnie answered, which was pertinent to nothing. She knew she was struggling. But, truth be told, she was more than a tiny bit fed up with this man's questions.

'I know that!' he clipped. 'I was late getting here myself.'

Oh, grief, he was growing narky again! For herself, she didn't give a button. But for Johnny... Even if she did feel like wringing her brother's neck for what he had done, she knew she would not let him down.

'The fog was dreadful, wasn't it?' she commented pleasantly. Deaf ears. Leon Beaumont ignored her pleasant comment. 'Actually, I somehow didn't expect you to be here until today—er—the fog and everything,' she added lamely. 'Um, you must have put your car away in the garage.' She came to an end to see that he had clearly heard quite enough of her rambling on.

'Just what *are* you doing here?' he challenged aggressively. 'And how the hell did you get in?'

Tell him, urged her true self. And she knew she would derive a great deal of satisfaction from doing just that. But—Johnny... Somehow, just to tell this man that his assistant was her brother seemed like letting Johnny down. 'Oh—sorry,' she apologised, racking her brains. 'Didn't I say?' What? What? What? 'There's a spare key hidden in the pyracantha bush by the tool shed. Er—Mrs Lloyd can't come after all—' Varnie broke off, her brain racing. 'I'm here as her replacement.' Had she actually just said that? She hadn't—had she?

Looking at Leon Beaumont, Varnie saw that he didn't appear to believe it either. He cast an eye over her trim figure, in her casual but obviously good clothes, and bluntly, scepticism rife again, questioned, 'You're here to do domestic work?'

Varnie, used as she was to looking out for her brother, couldn't see what other choice she had. 'Yes,' she confirmed.

His answer was to take hold of both her delicate hands. She immediately wanted to snatch her hands back, but by effort of will managed to stay still. She did not often have a manicure, but she had been going to go on holiday, for goodness' sake, with someone she had up until yesterday thought of as someone a bit special. So why wouldn't she go the whole hog and have her hands and nails professionally attended to?

'These hands have never known hard work,' he stated, tossing them disgustedly away from him.

'Yes, they have!' she argued.

'You've skivvied?' So absurd did the notion seem to appear to be to him, he looked as though he might burst out laughing. He didn't.

'I have!'

'It looks like it.'

'I was in the hotel trade!' she defended, while hardly knowing why she was bothering. 'I've worked all areas when required—chambermaid, cleaner, chef, secretary, accountant,' she enumerated.

'You were learning the hotel business?' He seemed to reconsider. 'So what happened?' he wanted to know.

'The—er…' Oh, heavens, how much had Johnny told him? 'The hotel sold out to a bigger chain,' she lied. 'There were two of us doing the same job. I—er—sort of lost out.'

'You were sacked!'

Oh, how she would like to poke him in the eye—both eyes, come to that. 'Not sacked. They've said they'll give me a splendid reference.' She had been in charge of that sort of thing; she could write *herself* a super reference if need be. Though of course a reference wouldn't be needed for casual work.

'So when this Mrs Lloyd told Metcalfe she couldn't come, he rang and asked you to come and help out?' he asked, looking not taken in for a second.

'That's about it,' Varnie answered. What on earth was she doing? While she wanted to stay on at Aldwyn House, no way did she want to stay here *with him*! And no way did she want to stay and, worse, work for the wretched man.

'Thanks, but no thanks.' He declined an offer that she was not altogether sure she had made anyway.

'Why not?' Why was she arguing? Johnny—must keep Johnny to the forefront of her mind. Part of being a sister meant looking out for one's sibling—no matter how infuriating that sibling could be at times.

For a moment it did not look as though Leon Beaumont would deign to answer. Then, abruptly, 'I don't take favours,' he said curtly.

Good! Johnny! Damn. 'It's you who'll be doing me a favour,' she said in a rush—Johnny Metcalfe, you owe me, big-time. 'I'm out of a job and I've nowhere to live until I hear from my live-in job applications,' she lied sorrowfully.

Leon Beaumont looked as if to say, Tough. Oh, how she'd delight in kicking him out. Did Johnny really, really want to keep his job? 'You intend to "live-in"?' Beaumont asked harshly. 'You want to be a...' he paused '...a "live-in" skivvy?' he enquired deliberately.

Oh, to thump his head! 'The nearest town is miles away,' she controlled herself to explain.

'You didn't come here on your bike—there's a car parked out there.'

Clearly this man did not miss much. She'd had it with him. I tried, Johnny, I tried. 'So I'll leave!' she answered snappily—and with no little amazement. She had been going to throw this man out, for goodness' sake, and here she was, saying that *she* was going to leave! Johnny, of course. A part of his job appeared to be to find this womanising swine a bolthole when his womanising backfired on him. Well, Johnny had been efficient—he *had* found him that bolthole—nobody was likely to find Beaumont here.

She sighed heavily, and was about to get out of there when she found that Leon Beaumont had misinterpreted the reason for her sigh. He thought she was sighing because she was homeless and had nowhere to go. She guessed it was that, but didn't thank him for it when suddenly he seemed to relent in his tough stance.

But his tone was curt, nevertheless, when he stated abruptly, 'You can stay and earn your keep—with certain conditions.'

Huh! Big of you! I own this place! Johnny? Always Johnny. She lowered her glance so Beaumont should not see the enmity in her eyes. 'Anything you say,' she answered meekly.

There was a moment of silence, as if he either didn't care for her meekness or did not believe in it. But he was soon sharply itemising. 'One, you tell anyone I'm here—just so much as a whispered hint—and you're out. Got that?'

She knew he meant the press, if they came sniffing around. They must have been 'doorstepping' him to have got that picture of him decking Neville King. 'You don't want anyone to know you're here?' she asked innocently. 'I saw a picture of you in the paper yesterday. Are you afraid of that woman's husband...?' She didn't finish, and he didn't bother to dignify her absurd question with an answer.

'I want no company but my own,' he told her forthrightly.

'You're off women too?'

'In spades!' he retorted, and she could see that he meant it. 'Which leads me to the second condition. *You* stay out of my bedroom!'

Oh, the arrogance of it! How she managed to hold down some snappy comment she had no idea. But she did, to ask nicely, 'You'll manage to make your own bed?'

He gave her a speaking look. She waited to be hired or fired. 'Get my breakfast!' he ordered.

Get it yourself, sprang to mind. But by the look of it, whether she wanted it or not—and she did not—she had been hired. 'Three bags full, sir,' she retorted, her phoney meekness short-lived as, his instructions given, he strode out.

Varnie went to her grandfather's pantry to see what, if anything, there might be there that would in any way do for his lordship's breakfast.

As she had anticipated, unless he fancied canned mandarins followed by canned corned beef, there was nothing. She went to the drawing room, where she found her new and unwanted employer standing looking out of the window.

He was so not interested in her he did not even turn around. 'I shall have to go to the shops,' she announced bluntly.

He did turn then, favouring her with a brooding kind of look. 'Get me a newspaper,' he commanded, and, to her huge embarrassment, he took out his wallet, extracted some notes and, without a word, held them out to her.

She flushed scarlet. 'I don't want your money!' she erupted indignantly.

He stared at her in some surprise—surprise not only at her high colour but at her genuine indignation too. He seemed about to make some comment about both, but changed his mind to tell her bluntly, 'I don't want you paying for my breakfast.' And, ramming the money into her hand, 'Bring receipts,' he snarled, and, plainly fed up with her, left her standing there.

Varnie wondered if she would last the day without thumping him. Never had she met such a man. He could starve as far as she was concerned. But again her mutiny was squashed by thoughts of her dear—though not so dear at the moment—brother.

She knew then that she would do all she could not to, as it were, rock the boat for Johnny. She would, because he loved his job so well, and for once seemed settled in a career, try to put in a good word for him whenever she could. She would do a good job on his behalf too, as long as it lasted. She hoped it would not be for long. She looked at the money in her hands. Oh, grief, there was enough there to keep them in supplies for a month.

She felt better when common sense stirred to make her feel sure he had no intention of being away from his business for that long. She determined, however, that she would ask Beaumont just how long he was staying at her first opportunity.

Hoping that it would not be longer than for just a few days, she went upstairs to take a shower—it wouldn't hurt him to wait a little longer for his breakfast.

She heard him on the phone in her grandfather's study as she went by on her way out to her car. Darned cheek!

Though, in fairness, she supposed that since he was probably expecting to pay rent for this hideaway accommodation that his assistant had 'found' for him, Beaumont assumed he was renting the whole house—and that included the study.

Varnie bought sufficient supplies to last a week, and took her purchases back to her car. She was loading up the boot while musing that her grandfather's fridge-freezer would come in handy, when someone called her name.

She straightened up. 'Varnie Sutton!' exclaimed the wiry, fair-haired man standing there, a broad smile on his face.

'Russell Adams!' She smiled in return.

He caught a hold of her arms and bent and kissed her cheek. She had always liked Russell. He and his parents lived about a mile from Aldwyn House. He was the same age as Johnny, and they had spent some splendid childhood times together. Then he and Johnny had gone to university—Johnny had dropped out after a year—and they had seen less of Russell. She guessed it must be five years since she had last seen him.

'I heard about your grandfather,' Russell remarked. 'I'm sorry I couldn't come to his funeral to pay my respects. Working away,' he explained, but added quickly, 'Have you time for a coffee? We could catch up. Is Johnny with you?'

'I really should…' Get back, she would have said, only she suddenly felt quite happy to think of Beaumont back at Aldwyn House, waiting for his breakfast. 'Of course I've time,' she said brightly.

And over coffee she learned that Russell was now a qualified civil engineer whose work took him all over the place. He now lived in Caernarvon, but was here visiting his parents for a day or two. In the space of fifteen minutes Varnie learned that Russell was unmarried, but had once 'come close,' and that there was no one else he was interested in. Russell liked his job well enough, but sometimes fancied working at something different.

'How's Johnny doing? I expect he's married and settled down?'

'He's still single,' Varnie replied, hoping that he was settled, and realising that perhaps she should make more of an effort on his behalf. Perhaps try to get Leon Beaumont to see what a good assistant he had in her brother. Which reminded her—she'd better head back. This was no way to make sure Johnny kept his job. She had to be the best 'skivvy' going—this skivvy that Johnny had organised.

'And how about you?' Russell asked. 'Still breaking hearts, Varnie? Or do you have someone special in your life?'

Still breaking hearts? She was sure she never had. Though as she thought about someone special in her life it was Leon Beaumont and his need for sustenance that occupied her. And it was with quite a start that she all at once realised that thoughts of the person who yesterday had been the someone special in her life had been astonishingly absent!

'No one,' she answered, hiding her astonished feelings. 'But I think I'd better be going. It was lovely bumping into you ag—'

'How long are you here for?' Russell cut in.

'I'm not really sure,' she hedged, and stood up. She really should be getting back.

Russell walked to her car with her, suggesting that perhaps he might call and see her the next day. Varnie liked him very much, but was unsure of how she was going to cope being head cook and bottle-washer for Johnny's employer. And in any event Beaumont, who didn't want anyone to know where he was, would probably be furious should she have 'gentleman callers' turning up at his hideaway. Though hadn't Russell said he was only here for a day or so?

'I shall be pretty busy sorting out my grandfather's affairs,' Varnie invented, and kissed cheeks with Russell on parting. But she drove back to Aldwyn House still feeling very much shaken that, when she had believed she thought enough of Martin Walker to go on holiday with him he should, in less than twenty-four hours, barely figure in her thoughts!

Though when she considered the depths of his deception—he was a married man, for goodness' sake, deceiving his wife, the mother of his children—Varnie began to feel less astonished that he had killed stone-dead her feeling for him. No wonder he did not figure largely in her thoughts. She knew then that she had not loved him as much as she had thought. She had been stunned, and that was natural enough. Had felt sick and half a dozen other emotions. But any feelings she had thought she'd for him had died the moment he had acknowledged that he was married, yet had still thought she might go away with him when he lyingly told her he was getting a divorce.

She had thought she would find living with the knowledge of his deceit exceedingly painful, but in actual fact the only thing that was smarting was her pride that she had been so gullible. How could she have been so unworldly as not to smell something fishy when the only times she'd seen him had been when he was Cheltenham way on business? And that had always been in the week. True, she had worked peculiar hours too. But really—and dim wasn't the word for it—only now did the fact that in all the months she had known him never once had they both had a weekend free at the same time. Even one time when he was supposed to be free, and she'd managed to swap duties and arranged to see him, he had rung at the last minute to say that something had cropped up. Of course it had—his wife and children!

Varnie put him from her mind, realising that perhaps she had Leon Beaumont to thank that Martin Walker hadn't spent the whole of that morning occupying her head. For goodness' sake, it wasn't every day that she strolled naked into some man's bedroom! That was certainly enough to block off all thoughts of some other man. And that was without his overbearing attitude and all that followed. The arrogant...

Varnie calmed down. Johnny. She must keep that clever brother, but—as his father said—often without a grain of sense, to the forefront of her mind. He did not deserve her consideration after what he had done; how dared he hand over his key to *her* property and invite his boss to use the place as his own? But Johnny did so love his job, and wanted desperately to keep it, and he was her brother and, as her brother, the rights and wrongs of it just didn't come into it.

That being so, Varnie decided she must make the best of a bad job. She did not want Beaumont in her house, but since, she reluctantly faced, she could not throw him out if Johnny was to keep his job, she would allow him to stay— and only hope it wouldn't be for more than a day or so.

She pulled up her car to the side of the house and started to extract the groceries while at the same time deciding that, since it looked as though she was going to have to put up with him, she might as well be nice to Beaumont. No, not Beaumont—Leon.

He came into the kitchen just as she placed her first three carriers down on the kitchen table. 'You took your time!' he opened curtly.

She felt her hackles go on the incline. Be nice. Be nice. She smiled. 'I met a friend. We had coffee,' she replied pleasantly, and was about to add that she'd have brunch ready in next to no time when he butted in—a habit of his she had noticed and didn't very much care for.

'You know someone here?' he questioned sharply.

She very nearly slipped up and said of course she did, that she had spent all her childhood holidays here. In time, she remembered. 'I did tell you I'd been here before,' she stated quietly.

'With Metcalfe?'

'Naturally. He—um—rented this place before.'

'How well do you know him?' Leon Beaumont was interested in knowing.

Oh, you'd be surprised. She toyed briefly with the idea of confessing that Johnny was her brother, her stepbrother, but only briefly. Her being here, skivvying, was her attempt to prove to Leon just how very efficient his assistant was. How, when Mrs Lloyd could not make it, his resourceful and worthwhile assistant had speedily found a replacement to cook and clean for him. Besides, this man didn't take favours. No, she definitely could not tell him that his assistant was her brother. So, in answer to his question of how well she knew him, she had to settle for, 'Very well.'

'You and he are an item?'

'No!' she answered, more sharply than she'd meant.

'You've slept with him?' he questioned shortly.

'Do I ask you whom you've slept with?' she retaliated. The sauce of it!

'So you have?'

A childhood memory—a sweet childhood memory—of her being very upset one time. A stray cat had been run over just outside. She had been horrified and dreadfully tearful. She had been awake in the night, sobbing, and Johnny had come from his room—he'd have been about eight at the time. 'Don't cry, Varnie,' he'd begged, and had climbed into her bed and cuddled her better. They had both dropped off to sleep. Who could help but love him? She smiled at the fond memory. 'Yes,' she agreed, 'I've slept with him.'

'Obviously not a lasting experience,' Leon Beaumont answered with a dismissive kind of a grunt—inferring, she felt, that his assistant had dumped her when he had grown tired of her.

'Perhaps you'll feel sweeter when you've got something in your stomach,' she said nicely—lead shot came to mind.

He gave her a nasty look and wandered away, and in between stowing the shopping Varnie cooked him bacon, eggs and beans. In the hope that his arteries were clogging up, she added a piece of fried bread.

The meal was almost ready when she went to lay a place in the dining room. Beaumont came out of the study and saw her with the tray in her hands. 'I'll eat in the kitchen,' he decided, and she was sure he only said it to be difficult. Still, if he wanted to eat with what he thought was the hired help, who was she to say he couldn't?

She had thought the meal would be eaten with not a word being exchanged. But, sitting at one end of the scrubbed-top kitchen table, a cloth hastily thrown over it, he at the other end, she had barely cut into her bacon when to her surprise he enquired, 'Where do you come from?'

Varnie popped a morsel of bacon in her mouth, and under cover of chewing it, and emptying her mouth before speaking, cogitated on her answer. Had Johnny, during the miles he had driven him around the country, told him anything at all about his family? Or had Beaumont been occupied with work the whole of the time?

'Gloucestershire.' She decided to risk it. Her brother had lived in London for some years now.

'Where did you meet Metcalfe?' he wanted to know.

'He stayed at a hotel I worked at one time.' And she'd thought she hated liars!

Though of course Johnny *had* stayed at the hotel. But why wouldn't he? Their parents had owned it. Leon Beaumont opened his mouth to ask another question she was sure she wouldn't want to answer either, but she butted in first. It made a change.

'Talking of staying, how long were you thinking of staying on here?' she asked, and felt herself go a touch pink. She saw his glance on her delicate colouring, saw his glance go to what had once been described as a very kissable mouth, and she hated him when he ignored her question and made an observation instead.

'You're looking guilty about something?' he questioned grimly. 'What have you done?'

'Nothing!' she denied hotly. 'Honestly, you're the most, most…' she got stuck for a word '…most I've ever met!' Oddly then, his lips twitched, as though she amused him. Though his smile never made it. Abruptly she dragged her eyes from his well-shaped mouth. 'It was a quite innocent question,' she defended. 'I like to know where I am. If I have some idea of how long you intend to be here, then I'll have some idea of what to do with regard to the catering arrangements.' She was starting to feel a fool. 'Just how long are you staying?' she demanded. As if she expected an answer! She didn't get one.

'I'm on holiday,' was as much as he revealed. And that annoyed her.

'It's November! Why can't you holiday abroad like everybody else?' she snapped, exasperated.

'I've done the ''abroad'' bit,' he answered, and while she was wondering what the penalty was for fratricide—she felt like murdering her brother—Beaumont went silkily on, 'You've got something against my holidaying here?'

Who am I to complain? I'm only the skivvy! This was helping Johnny keep his job? 'No, of course not,' she swallowed her ire. 'I feel very lucky that Johnny…' Bother, she should have said John. Too late now. 'Er—Johnny Metcalfe thought of me when he wanted emergency cover. It's just that I should hate to let him down should a job offer come before your—um—holiday is over. Naturally I'd honour my contract with John Metcalfe first. He was insistent that I didn't let you down…' Oh, grief, was she laying on John Metcalfe's efficient reliability too thickly? 'There's more bacon there if you'd like…'

'You sound as if you're fond of him, as if you'd do anything for him?'

Varnie had had quite enough of Beaumont's observations. 'Well, I've always found him to be a man of the highest integrity.' She found she was spreading more on—grief, she was sounding like a talking reference.

'You're in love with him?' Blunt, to the point.

'No, I'm not!' she denied, realising that perhaps she had been singing Johnny's praises a little too highly. She tried for the middle ground. 'He's a very nice person, that's all, and I'm very fond of him.'

'But not *in* love with him?'

Varnie gave him an exasperated look. 'I said not!' she exploded. And, before she could stop herself, 'And, contrary to your opinion that I might fancy you—I'm off men, quite severely, right now.' And, with barely veiled innuendo, 'In particular men to whom the state of marriage means nothing!' There, pick the bones out of that!

He did. But to her further annoyance chose not to see her remarks as a dig at him for his disgraceful goings-on—that woman—what was her name?—Antonia King—was still living with her husband, for goodness' sake. 'Some man refused to marry you?' Beaumont leaned back in his chair to enquire coolly.

Varnie sent him a filthy look for his trouble. She didn't mean *her*! She meant *him*! 'It didn't get that far,' she erupted. 'I found out he was married!' She looked away in disgust. Had she really openly just told Leon Beaumont that? For goodness' sake! Okay, she accepted that to be a successful businessman probably meant having an investigative mind, an enquiring mind, a mind that determined to find out that which he did not know. But...

He proved it. 'You dumped him?'

Honestly, this man! 'Quicker than that!' she snapped. And, having had quite sufficient of his company, thank you, she abruptly got to her feet. 'If you've had enough to eat, I'll wash these dishes,' she said shortly.

He carried his own used dishes over to the sink, but wasn't yet done with his questions, apparently. 'This man, the one you had coffee with—is he the married one who...?'

'I never said my friend was a man.'

Leon Beaumont looked loftily down at her. 'You're saying your friend was female?'

She felt a fool again. She did not like the feeling. 'Do you give all your—your staff this—um—third degree?' she questioned hostilely.

He smiled. He actually smiled. It did wonders for the mostly severe expression she was more used to. She wasn't sure that her heartbeats did not give a little flip—utter nonsense, of course—but it did make her see, as Johnny had told her, why women fell for him like ninepins. Not her, of course. Heaven forbid.

'Not all of them,' he drawled. 'But you're so delightful to wind up.'

The pig! He was baiting her for his own amusement! While she admitted that there was not very much going on around here in the way of entertainment, she did not take kindly to the fact that he was amusing himself by getting her to rise—that she was the star turn! How she hid the fact that she would like to crack the plate in her hands over his head, she did not know.

'Thanks a bunch!' she told him huffily. 'I'll let you know when dinner's ready.'

'Your friend knows you're here at Aldwyn House?' he stayed to enquire, ignoring her hint that she hoped not to see him again before dinner.

'I expect so,' she answered carefully.

'You didn't say what you were doing here?' Leon Beaumont's tone had hardened, as he reminded her how much he wanted his whereabouts kept secret.

For about two seconds she played with the idea of saying that she had. Then thoughts of Johnny were there again. Perishing brothers! 'No,' she replied. 'I didn't think you'd like me to tell him.'

'Are you having coffee with him again?' he wanted to

know, taking in his stride the information that her friend *had* been male, as he had thought.

She shook her head. 'Russell is returning to his home in Caernarvon soon,' she replied.

'Good!' Leon Beaumont grunted, and, taking up the newspaper from the top of one of the units, where she had put it, he went casually out from the kitchen.

Varnie did not mistake that that 'Good!' was anything other than good because it meant there was someone less for her to blab to about his whereabouts. The man did not care a jot how many men she had coffee with, that much was certain. His privacy was all that concerned him. She wouldn't have it any other way.

CHAPTER THREE

SOMEHOW the weekend passed without Varnie putting rat poison in Leon Beaumont's food. They were sparky with each other—she couldn't always remember to be nice.

Well, who would? she thought mutinously on more than one occasion. He still did not seem totally convinced that she wasn't there trying to make capital of the situation of them being under the same roof alone together. Huh!

She sat in front of her dressing table mirror on Monday morning and brushed her long blonde hair, then flipped it up into an elegant bun. She allowed her large sea-green eyes to study her dainty features and clear complexion, then took her eyes from the mirror to stare down at her well-kept hands and long fingers with their neat and equally well-kept nails. Then had to suppose that in all honesty she was not your general picture of an everyday 'skivvy'.

Varnie left her room, never more grateful that her grandfather had thought to install a computer in his study. Not so far as she knew that he had used it for any business purpose, but she knew he had spent many a happy hour playing either bridge or chess on it. But the machine came in useful for getting Leon Beaumont out of her hair. What work he could do at weekends she had no idea, but the computer had been on when she had taken him in a cup of coffee yesterday morning. And he had been playing neither bridge nor chess, but had had a screen full of matter that was way past her comprehension. With luck the computer would keep him occupied for all of this day too.

She was always astir at six. He was downstairs before her and already in the kitchen drinking coffee. He wasn't mean,

44

she'd give him that, when, not bothering to ask if she wanted one, he poured her a cup of coffee.

'Thanks,' she said, and, remembering her place, 'Good morning,' she added pleasantly. Which turned out to be a bit of a wasted effort when he ignored her and went, carrying his coffee, out through the kitchen door. 'Suit yourself!' she addressed his departing back.

'Good morning!' sailed back to her—and, oddly, she had to laugh.

And so the day began. Leon Beaumont spent a great deal of his day working in the study and she barely saw him. He made several telephone calls and, when she rushed to answer the phone so that it should not disturb him, she found that he had answered the phone first and that the call was for him.

It would not have been for her anyway, she belatedly realised, because no one but Russell Adams knew that she was there. And Russell was probably back in Caernarvon by now. So Varnie got on with the job she was supposed to be there to do, and cleaned that which had to be cleaned, left fresh towels outside her 'employer's' door, and cooked that which had to be cooked. She went to bed that night feeling not as satisfied with her day's work as she should have been, and somehow feeling more than a little fed-up.

She was still feeling the same when she got up the next morning and went down the stairs, musing that her only reason for coming here had been so that her parents should enjoy the tranquillity of their retirement and not be upset that she was upset.

But, and she could hardly believe it, she did not feel as emotionally broken as she had supposed she would when the numbness of Martin Walker's dreadful deceit had worn off. What she did feel was disgusted with him, and disbelieving of her own naivety. So—if there was nothing for her parents to be upset about—what in creation was she doing here? Suddenly she realised that—she could go home!

Leon was in the kitchen. He poured her a cup of coffee and, impulsively, before she could think it through, she blurted out, 'Would it put you out too much if I left?'

He was standing by the draining board and studied her with cool grey eyes. 'Good morning,' he replied, and took a swig of his coffee. Her lips twitched, but if he noticed he paid no heed, but told her easily, 'I wouldn't be at all put out. You're quite free to go whenever you wish.'

Truly, he didn't give a light. But something, she knew not what, but something in the way he said it caused her to hesitate. And when she should have been skipping up the stairs to gather her belongings together, she stayed. Stayed to question, 'You're sure you don't mind?'

'I've said so,' he answered curtly. 'Though if you're in touch with your friend Metcalfe before I am you might tell him to take my name off his CV.'

Varnie's mouth fell open in shock. What broader hint than that did she need that, should she leave, then Johnny would be leaving his employ too, *tout de suite*! He was as good as saying that if she left him in the lurch—domestic-wise—there would be no point in John Metcalfe applying to the company for a reference! What Leon Beaumont was saying was tantamount to informing her that Johnny's job was on the line here. That if she did not stay to do the job his assistant had hired her to do, then that said assistant could wave goodbye to his job too.

'But—that's—that's blackmail!' she gasped, realising then that he must have formed the opinion that she was fond enough of his assistant to not want to lose him his job.

'You reckon?' he drawled.

She stared at him, dumbstruck. 'But—but you didn't want me here anyway!' she protested. 'On Saturday you were in two minds about throwing me out!' How long ago Saturday seemed—she had been on the point of throwing *him* out. Oh, if only.

'Your housekeeping skills aren't bad, and you're a halfway decent cook,' he commented, unmoved. And while she looked at him incredulously that he was a man who so obviously enjoyed his creature comforts he was prepared to blackmail her to keep them, he sauntered, coffee in hand, to boot up the computer—presumably to check on any overnight happenings in his international company.

Rat poison was too good for him! With hate in her heart Varnie silently swore that if the chance ever came for her to do Beaumont one in the eye she would grab it with both hands.

Varnie mutinied against him for the rest of the morning. The post came—there was mail for him. She let him come and find it on the hall table himself. She was his cook and cleaner, not his secretary. Though, seeing the typed name L. Beaumont, it showed that he must have acquainted someone with where he was hiding away. On thinking about it, she rather supposed that a man in his position with a company to run could hardly disappear from the face of the earth for weeks on end.

Weeks on end! Surely not! Oh, grief, she hoped not. He couldn't possibly leave his business for that long—could he? She had been giving serious thought about making her own career and wanted to get on with it—*now*.

She felt defeated suddenly. Johnny planned to be away a whole month. A whole month! No! Leon Beaumont couldn't plan to be here that long? Well, she wasn't staying here all that time! For one thing her parents were expecting her home a week next Saturday. No way was she staying here any longer than that, that was for definite.

All Leon had wanted for lunch yesterday had been a sandwich. He could have the same today, she decided, still feeling extremely rebellious against the man—how dared he blackmail her into staying? On the other hand—how dared she go?

It slowly began to dawn on her then that she could not go home yet anyway. How could she? While she would be able to put her parents' minds at rest that she was not as upset as she had envisaged to have broken with Martin Walker—what on earth had there been to break? He was married, for goodness' sake—how could she tell them what Johnny had done? True, they were used to his misdemeanours—Johnny had been a bit of a trial from an early age, always up to something. He had been eleven when he had sold his bicycle to fund his temporary obsession with some amusement arcade. When the dust had settled, and their parents had calmly pointed out to him that it was dishonest to do such a thing, he had replied with logic there was no arguing with that, as the bicycle was their birthday present to him, he thought it was his, and his to do with as he wished.

All other misdemeanours aside, never before had he rented out someone else's property, albeit his sister's. Varnie had covered for him countless times, but her mother seemed to have grown a special antenna where she was concerned, and had a foolproof instinct whenever her daughter tried to be evasive. From experience she seemed to nose out when Johnny had been up to something—and when Varnie was trying to protect him—and she rarely got it wrong.

While Varnie knew herself a hopeless liar, and could not lie to her parents and thereby had to accept that she could not go home just yet anyway, she had no such problems in lying to Beaumont. But then, he did not deserve any better. Womanising swine! No woman was safe from him, except maybe her, but then she was only the skivvy.

He came out from the study at lunchtime, spotted the mail on the hall table and, Varnie noted, happening to be in the hall at the same time, did not seem a happy bunny.

'How long has this been here?' he demanded.

Varnie looked at him guilelessly from her big sea-green eyes. 'Is it important?' she asked sweetly. And, going to the drawing room door, 'I've put your snack in here. I'll just get you some coffee.' She received a grunt by way of a reply.

She went back to the kitchen knowing full well that she was being petty in the extreme. But it was amazing how good being petty made her feel. Womanising, blackmailing toad, he did not deserve better.

He was standing staring out of one of the long drawing room windows when she returned with his coffee. Placing the tray down on a low table, she thought about asking if he would like her to pour, before deciding that he was big enough to do that for himself. Then she forgot every bit about coffee when she heard him mutter some kind of oath.

She looked over to him, and was glad to see that the oath was not aimed at her. He was still looking out of the window, she observed, only now, as she went over to see what he was swearing about, she saw that it wasn't the leaf-strewn neglected garden he was looking at, but the car that had stopped at the end of the drive. Plainly he recognised the car—and its female driver. Equally plainly, he was not thrilled.

Varnie was quite impressed. Unless he had been born a grumpy old devil, and according to her brother Leon Beaumont had enough charm to have women ready to lie down and die for him, then she wasn't the only one to upset Beaumont's apple cart.

'Friend or foe?' she asked innocently.

'Bloody woman!' he snarled.

'*Moi?*' Varnie queried, enjoying herself.

'Short of getting a court order to get her to leave me alone, I've told her every way I know how that I'm not interested!' he rapped, as an elegant brunette got out of car and began to unto the gates at the bottom on the drive that had been closed since Varnie had returned from shopping on Saturday.

The woman got back into her car and steered it up the drive. They were standing back from the window, and where she had parked they could see her but she could not see them.

Then something clicked for Varnie. 'Antonia King!' she exclaimed.

'You know her?' He rounded on her furiously. 'You told her I was here?' he accused blisteringly.

'She's very photogenic!' Varnie snapped right back. 'The only time I saw her was when her picture was in the paper. Perhaps she's come to ask you to stop thumping her husband!' she commented artlessly, and was on the receiving end of a nasty look for her trouble.

'Damn you, damn her, and damn her husband!' he snarled. 'I'm sick of it.' And, in no uncertain terms, 'Go and tell her to clear off!' he ordered.

Varnie stared at him in amazement. 'Suddenly I'm elevated from household drudge and halfway decent cook to the great and dizzying heights of your social secretary? Do your own dirty work!' Varnie erupted. 'Tell her yourself!'

'I will!' he barked. 'I've had it with her—she's out!' With that he went striding towards the door.

Only just then Varnie recalled the press report saying that Antonia King worked for him. 'Just a minute!' she called urgently.

He stopped, half turned. 'What?' he barked, looking as impatient as blazes.

'She works for you, doesn't she?'

'She did,' he agreed succinctly. 'She's just about to get fired!'

'Don't do that!' Varnie exclaimed impulsively. Leon Beaumont looked at her as if demanding to know who she thought she was to tell him how to run his company, and Varnie hurried on, 'She must be good at her job or she wouldn't be one of your executives.'

'She wouldn't have been promoted if she wasn't up to it,' he agreed coldly, but went on angrily, 'I've had enough. This has to stop now. It's bloody ridiculous! All I did was a bit of PR management, to encourage her when she was first upgraded to the top floor, and the stupid woman seems to think it's personal. I've had it with clinging women—she's out!' With that he was at the door.

'Stop!' Varnie cried, feeling certain that despite what he had said no woman would latch on to him from just a little PR. Public relations, my foot. He must have encouraged her more than that, and now the poor woman was going to lose her job, her career. 'I'll do it—tell her to go. I'll tell her to leave you alone—for ever,' Varnie said.

Leon Beaumont paused to give her a suspicious look. 'Why?' he asked. 'Less than a minute ago you were all for me doing my own ''dirty work''.'

'A minute ago I didn't know you intended to sack her,' Varnie explained. 'I've been thinking just lately in terms of building some kind of career for myself, and—'

'In the hotel trade?'

He never forgot a thing, obviously. She'd have to try and remember what lies she told him. 'It depends what offers I get from my job applications. I might try something different—er—if I can get fixed up with accommodation.' She started to get hot. 'The thing is...' She thought Antonia King to be around thirty. 'I shouldn't like to be seven or eight years into my career only to be dismissed because, with nothing wrong with my work, I had a crush on my boss.'

'Hmph!' He did not think much of her reasoning, but at least he wasn't striding off to tell Antonia King to find employment elsewhere. 'The only crush she's got is on my wallet.'

Just then Antonia King started knocking on the front door—she must have been ringing the bell, only to find it did not work, Varnie realised. Grandfather Sutton had disconnected it when its ringing interfered with his computer concentration.

'I've had it up to here with women,' Leon Beaumont

stated grimly, a hand measuring up to his throat. And, thoroughly disgruntled, 'I'm going back to work!'

Varnie, with a small feeling of triumph, realised she had won a reprieve for the female executive. 'What shall I tell her?' she asked, smiling.

'Tell her what the hell you like. Just make it clear that if she comes here again—or for that matter anywhere near me that isn't connected with business—she's out!'

With that he went back to the study. Varnie heard the thud of the study door. Oh, my word, guess who didn't want to be disturbed? She glanced at the snack she had prepared for him. Quite clearly someone was off their food.

The sound of Antonia King again knocking on the woodwork sent Varnie hurrying to answer the door. If she didn't Leon would come from the study and give the poor woman what for.

She pulled back the door and spotted that the elegant brunette seemed surprised to see her. 'Yes?' Varnie enquired.

Antonia King gave her an impatient look—clearly she did not care to be kept waiting. 'This *is* Aldwyn House?' she demanded haughtily—and Varnie did not care very much for her superior attitude. Poor woman? Forget it.

'It is,' she replied, masking her feelings. 'What can I do for you?'

'I've come to see Mr Beaumont!' she snapped, her demeanour so staggeringly dismissive of her that Varnie could hardly believe it.

Somehow, though, she managed to hold back on some short and sharp comment to say instead, 'I'm afraid he's not available to see anyone. I can give him a message if you'd like to—'

'I'll come in and wait,' Antonia King decided, and, without waiting to be invited, was ready to push her way in.

Varnie did not like it. And it had nothing to do with Leon Beaumont wanting his privacy. She didn't like this woman's attitude, and she was just a little fed up with people treating what was after all her property as though it belonged to them.

'I'm sorry. That just isn't convenient!' she said coolly, moving to block the way. Had the woman's manner been a little different she might well have invited her in for some refreshment after her drive—presumably she had driven down from London—but she could jolly well go and have a coffee some place else.

'Who are you?' Antonia King interrogated tartly.

'I live here,' Varnie answered shortly, and saw the woman blink in astonishment. A second later and Varnie was astonished herself when it became clear just why Antonia King was so astonished.

'You're living with Leon?' she gasped.

Varnie was instinctively ready to deny the interpretation she read in the question. Though in actual fact she realised that she *was* living with him—if not in the way Antonia King implied. Suddenly Varnie remembered how, only that morning, she had vowed that if ever she had the chance to do Beaumont one in the eye she would grab it with both hands. He would just love it, wouldn't he, this man who was off women—in spades—if she told this woman that she and he—they—were a cosy twosome?

Varnie looked at her and saw no softness in her, this woman who had a husband and yet was after Leon Beaumont—and his wallet. 'Well, actually, yes, we do live together,' she told her. 'But Leon prefers us to keep it—er—private—um—quiet.' Quiet? He'd bellow and hit the roof when she relayed this conversation back to him.

'You're his mistress?' Antonia King asked, thoroughly taken aback.

'I like to think of myself more as his partner. Mistress is such an old hat word these days, wouldn't you agree?' And, not waiting for her to agree or not, 'I really shouldn't be discussing on the doorstep what is so very personal to my

darling—' she nearly choked on the word '—and me. Leon
is truly busy. If you—'

'You're lovers? That's what you're saying? You and
Leon…?'

'I'm sorry. I don't even know your name, and I really
can't—'

'I want to see him,' Antonia King insisted.

Good grief, this woman was a leech! Anybody else would
have slunk off long ago. 'I'll tell him you called. What
name—'

'How long have you and he been together?' the other
woman wanted to know—and Varnie was beginning to find
her tedious.

'Long enough to know that we care deeply for each
other.'

'Leon's in love with you?'

Desperately—he'll probably slit my throat when I go
back and tell him this little lot. 'Not that it's any business
of yours. But, yes—and it surprised me too,' Varnie inserted
when the other woman gave her a hard stare. 'Leon is in
love with me—quite madly in love with me, so he says.'
And, feeling she was going to gag if she said any more in
the same vein, 'Now, if you'd like to tell me your name and
give me a message for Leon…'

The message she received was Antonia King giving her
a venomous look of seething dislike before, without another
word, she turned about and went back to her car.

Oh, heavens! Varnie watched as the woman started her
car and went speeding to the end of the drive. She departed
the property without bothering to stop and close the gates
behind her.

Varnie fancied a breath of fresh air and took a walk to
the end of the drive. She closed the gates and, reviewing
what she had done, felt very much like carrying on walking.
Somehow it didn't seem as amusing now as it had at
the time.

Reluctantly she realised that she had better go back and face the music. Leon Beaumont was going to be as mad as blazes when she told him that she had got rid of his 'stalker'—and just how she had done it.

The door to the study was still shut. Varnie debated whether to leave telling him exactly how she had got rid of the woman whom he was convinced had more interest in his money than him. Perhaps she would go and prepare the evening meal first.

Oh, don't be such a coward. He can't kill you! Still the same, Varnie ignored the study and went into the drawing room. She pondered if what she had done constituted a good reason for him to dismiss Johnny from his employ, but decided it did not. In all fairness there was no way, just because she had claimed to be Leon Beaumont's live-in lover, that he could fire Johnny. She was still, after all, doing the job Johnny had supposedly hired her to do.

Better go and get it over with. She spotted the sandwiches she had prepared. Luckily she had covered them with a napkin or by now they would have been curling at the edges.

Deciding to make fresh coffee later, she picked up the sandwich tray and left the drawing room. She considered giving a courteous tap on the study door, as she always had before, but an instant later rebellion struck. This was her house, for goodness' sake. He was the interloper, not her!

Varnie was glad to feel mutinous; it made what she had done seem funny again. Without pausing to knock, she entered her grandfather's study. Leon Beaumont was engrossed with what the computer screen had to offer.

'I thought you might be hungry,' she lied, finding some space on the large desk and placing the sandwiches down. He looked up. She smiled. 'I'll make some fresh coffee.' He did not answer. She turned away. But then knew she wasn't going to keep this bottled up. 'Your visitor departed, by the way,' she informed him, turning back. She saw she had his attention. 'I don't think you'll have any more trouble there,' she announced.

Leon favoured her with an unsmiling look. 'I find that hard to believe,' he grated. 'I've tried every diplomatic—and not so diplomatic—way I know to get that result.'

Varnie smiled again. 'Ah, but there was one way you didn't think to try,' she said sweetly.

'Oh, to have your superior brain,' he mocked.

Bubbles to him. He annoyed her—so what else was new? She headed for the door.

'You're not going to leave it there, I trust?'

She turned again. And it gave her tremendous pleasure to be able to report, 'Mrs King was so determined to see you that—purely in the interests of her keeping her job, of course—I told her that you and I were—partners.'

'Partners?' he echoed. Clearly he was not believing his hearing.

'Live-in lovers,' Varnie answered prettily.

'You told her—'

Quiet before the storm! Varnie got in quickly, 'I told her that you were madly in love with me.'

'You did *what*?' he roared, and was on his feet.

Oh, my word, it was worth it. 'I knew you'd be pleased.' She stood her ground, even though Leon Beaumont came and stood over her—she had a feeling she was close to being grabbed by her ankles and swung around the study by her feet.

'Why, you conniving little—'

'Conniving?' she cut in, starting to get angry at being so accused.

'I told you, I specifically told you, that I was off all women—'

'I know—in spades,' she butted in.

'And that included you. If you think for one minute that, having aligned yourself with me, having broadcast that you and I are lovers, it will get you anywhere with me, then you can—'

'Why, you miserable—miserable...' there wasn't a name bad enough for him '...toad!' she erupted. The cheek of the man! The insufferable... 'I wouldn't fancy you if you were the last man breathing.'

'You're just as bad as she is.'

'For your information, I've had it up to here too—with men!'

'I warned you not to take advantage of this situation.'

'You're all a bunch of—' She broke off. They both seemed to be having their own individual argument here. 'If you didn't want her to find you—and in my view the woman shows extremely poor taste—why the devil did you give her this address?'

Leon Beaumont threw Varnie a look of disgust, but had reined in his fury when he clipped, 'I didn't. She went to see Evelyn Douglas, my PA, yesterday. Evelyn had an envelope on her desk addressed to me here that she intended to post personally. She rang me to say Antonia King had seen it before she could cover it up. I feared I might expect a visit.'

'What it is to be popular!' Varnie offered sarcastically. And, still angry at being accused of trying to get her hooks into him, 'Sort your own love-life out, Beaumont. Should Antonia King call again I shall take great delight in telling her that you're free and that she's welcome to you.'

With that she went storming out from the study. That man! She was going to leave! She'd had it with him. How dared he accuse her of wanting to 'get somewhere' with him? Why, he was as good as accusing her of having designs on his wallet!

Varnie stormed upstairs to pack. Never had she met such a man. Why, she was all of a tremble just from having to speak to him. No man had ever put her into this state before—and that included Martin Walker.

Up in her room, she took down her suitcase and had half filled it before the name Johnny came winging into her head. Oh, confound it! How could she leave? She slumped down in her bedroom chair. Then found that she couldn't sit still.

She went charging down the stairs again and, not thinking to restart a bad habit, declined to knock on the study door, but went barging straight in. Leon Beaumont glanced up, but she wasn't waiting for anything he might have to say but at once she demanded, 'Are you expecting me to leave, or what?'

Grey eyes studied sparking sea-green ones. He shrugged. 'Suit yourself.'

Good! No, not good. 'And if I go—what about John Metcalfe?' she questioned shortly.

Leon Beaumont smiled a smile she had no belief in. 'I'm surprised you need to ask,' he drawled.

The pig! The swine! The worm! For about five seconds they stared into each other's eyes—she furious, he, to her chagrin, slightly amused. 'Right,' she snapped, with no idea what she meant to convey by the word.

She turned to leave, but could have turned back to thump him when, addressing her back, he reminded her silkily, 'You won't forget about my coffee?'

Varnie got out of there. They were fairly isolated at Aldwyn House. Were she to kill him it could be weeks before his body was found. It was a pleasing thought.

She went mutinously along to the kitchen—though not to make his coffee. He could whistle for that. That 'I'm surprised you need to ask' had said it all. If she walked out, Johnny could say goodbye to the job he loved so much.

Varnie was still in the kitchen when the phone rang. She glanced at the kitchen phone but otherwise ignored it. It would be for his lordship. She hoped it was Antonia King, ringing to give him some verbal earache. To think she had actually tried to protect him from that vulture of a woman! Varnie hoped she got him—that would serve him right.

Though that wasn't such a happy prospect for Antonia King's husband, Neville.

The kitchen door opened. Leon Beaumont came in. 'There's a call for you!' he said shortly.

Sorry to interrupt, I'm sure. 'Who is it?' she asked bluntly.

'Who have you told you're here?' he countered.

Give me strength. She dried her hands and went over to the kitchen phone. She glanced meaningfully back at Leon—he did not take the hint—he wasn't going anywhere.

Varnie chalked up another crime at his door and picked up the phone. 'Hello?' she said.

'Who was that?' asked a vaguely familiar voice.

'Who is this?' she asked in return.

'Russell,' he answered. 'Russell Adams.'

'Oh, hello, Russell. How's Caernarvon?'

'I'm back at my parents'. I forgot my shaving gear. It was a good excuse to come back and see if you're free to come out for a meal tonight?'

'I—er...'

'Say yes. You can't spend all your time sorting your grandfather's affairs.'

Varnie held the phone closer to her ear, just in case Leon caught a whisper of any one word and his astute mind went to work. For that same reason, and because she was afraid that she might slip up and say something she didn't mean to say, she wanted this call to end speedily.

'That wasn't your boyfriend who answered, was it?' Russell thought to question as an afterthought.

'Good heavens, no. Just a friend of Johnny's who stopped by for a cup of tea.' Oh, heck. She could feel herself getting all hot and bothered—she hadn't meant to mention Johnny's name. 'Where shall I meet you?' she quickly asked.

'You'll come! Great! I'll come and pick you up. Shall we say—'

'I think it will be better if I drive myself,' she interrupted.

She didn't think Mr Beaumont would take kindly to her friends calling at his holiday hideaway. Not that she thought it would matter much who knew where he was now that Avaricious Antonia had run him to earth. Not, come to think of it, that Leon Beaumont was having much of a holiday either. He hadn't stopped working since he'd got here!

Russell said he'd book a table at a hotel they both knew, and they arranged to meet in the car park of the hotel at seven-thirty. Varnie was glad to end the call.

To her surprise, Leon Beaumont went and filled the kettle and set it to boil. Clearly he was thirsty. Clearly she was not going to make him a drink. 'As "Johnny's friend", perhaps I should have that cup of tea,' he commented smoothly, when she just stood there looking at him.

'I didn't think you'd appreciate me telling Russell who you were and what you're doing here.'

'That's why you suggested you'd meet him rather than allow him to come here and collect you?'

'That, and the fact I didn't want to advertise that I'm being blackmailed to skivvy for the grouch of the year.'

'Hell's teeth!' His sharp exclamation shattered the air. 'Without question you are the most lippy female it has ever been my misfortune to meet!'

'Thank you,' she replied pleasantly. In her view Leon Beaumont didn't deserve any better. There was a lot she would do, a lot she would put up with from sisterly love, but being subservient was not one of them. But all at once she started to feel totally fed-up. 'Tea or coffee?' she asked shortly, going over to the work surfaces.

'Tea,' he elected. 'What happened to "I've had it up to here with men"?'

'Russell? He's a friend.'

'That's different?'

'Don't you know any women who are just friends and nothing more?' As she said it, Varnie studied the tall, good-looking man, virility exuding from every pore. She didn't wait for an answer. 'No, I don't suppose you do,' she said cryptically. And, to her amazement, he laughed. It wasn't prolonged laughter, but his eyes lit up, and as she looked at him Varnie felt quite breathless. Ridiculous! She coughed, feeling choked suddenly, and quickly, to cover her slip in mentioning Johnny and Russell knowing each other, 'Russell's a friend of Johnny's too—we all met up one time.' And, before Leon could make anything out of that, 'All right with you if I leave you a casserole to help yourself from when you're ready?'

She'd fully expected him to be difficult. But, to her surprise, 'I think I can manage that,' he agreed, paused for a moment, and then added, 'You'll be home before midnight, I take it?'

Varnie stared at him. Surely he wasn't telling her to be back before the clock struck twelve? 'I must remember to wear my glass slippers!' she retorted, and left him to make his own tea.

In her room, however, she restlessly began to wonder what on earth was wrong with her. For heaven's sake, she was used to dealing with difficult people. You couldn't work in the hotel business and expect everyone who stayed with you to be all sweetness and light.

While it was true that Beaumont Esquire was very far from being all sweetness and light, why on earth was she so scratchy with him all the time? Hang on a minute—had she forgotten she was here as his housekeeper when that had never been her intention? To be fair to him, though, he did not know that, did he? He thought—and she had never said a peep to the contrary—had, in fact, fed him the information—that her being there was by prior arrangement with his assistant.

If she had to be scratchy with anybody, then surely it was his assistant she should be scratchy with. And would be, she determined, the very moment she set eyes on that diabolical brother of hers. Although she knew in advance from previous upsets with Johnny that she would soon forgive him and they would be back to normal in no time.

And anyhow—she roused her down-on-the-floor feelings—Leon Beaumont might think her the most lippy female it had ever been his misfortune to meet, but he wasn't exactly backwards when it came to forthrightly speaking his mind too!

Varnie was still feeling restless and out of sorts when, as she knew she had to, she returned downstairs to prepare her 'temporary employer' his evening meal. He was no longer in the kitchen and she was glad about that. She wasn't yet ready to see him again as she faced the fact that, while she was perfectly free to leave, no matter how fed up she was, because of Johnny there was no way that she *could* leave. Which in turn left her inwardly at war with herself, and outwardly at war with Leon Beaumont.

Her innate sense of fairness came and gave her a nudge. The poor man, he worked like a Trojan—he was supposed to be on holiday, for goodness' sake. Couldn't she be just a little bit nicer to him? She had to smile at that thought. As if he'd care! He would probably think she'd gone soft in the head if a day passed without her rearing up about something.

It had been like that from the beginning, she mused as, the casserole in the oven, the kitchen all clean and tidy, she went up to her room to shower. The thing was, though, that she was normally most even-tempered, and only ever reared up in anger in the direst of circumstances. She hadn't even gone for Martin Walker's jugular when she'd learned how he had taken her up the garden path. So what was so special about Leon Beaumont that she should react to him the way she did?

She had no idea, but as she showered and changed into smart trousers and a pale yellow silk shirt that particularly suited her she determined that she would try her hardest to be more her usual self with him in future. She would try to be nicer.

Going downstairs to check on the casserole, she saw that it was cooking nicely and should prove quite tasty. From the kitchen she went and laid the table in the dining room, and did a few more chores prior to returning to the kitchen. She hated unpunctuality, and planned to leave at seven so as to be in good time to meet Russell at seven-thirty.

At six-forty-five she went up to her room to check on her appearance and to pick up a jacket and her shoulder bag. She had previously heard the motor to the shower in the master bedroom. It had now stopped, and she felt she had given its occupant sufficient time to be respectably dressed. She went along and tapped on his door.

Leon opened it after a very short while. His dark hair was damp and he was buttoning up the front of his shirt, a smattering of dark hair showing through the opening. Her heart did such a ridiculous flip that for a moment she quite forgot exactly why she had come and knocked on his door in the first place.

What she did remember, most oddly, was the way he had warned her on Saturday morning to stay out of his bedroom. 'Don't worry, I don't want to come in,' she said, her voice strangely husky. She saw his lips twitch, her heart went soppy again—and she determinedly pulled herself together. 'Your dinner will be ready at seven-thirty. But it won't spoil if you want to eat a little later.'

'Thank you,' he answered politely, for all the world as if he had been giving himself the same 'be nicer' lecture she had not so long ago given herself.

'There's some cheesecake left from yesterday for afters. Or cheese and biscuits if you prefer.'

'I'm sure I won't go hungry,' he answered mildly.

She felt awkward, and she never felt awkward. 'I'll leave you to it, then,' she said, turning away.

'Have a pleasant evening,' he bade her.

A few minutes later she got into her car, telling herself that it would be good to have a night off. And she would enjoy spending some time with Russell Adams. Yet, most peculiarly, it was not thoughts of Russell that filled her head as she drove along. Nor did she think of Russell again until she drove into the hotel car park and she saw him there waiting for her. Her head had been much too fully occupied with thoughts of the man she had left behind at Aldwyn House. In fact, thoughts of Leon Beaumont seemed to have filled her mind constantly. Now, wasn't that the oddest thing?

CHAPTER FOUR

FOR once Varnie did not feel like getting up the next morning. She awoke at her normal time, but instead of leaving her bed to shower, prior to starting her day, she lay there and reviewed the events of the previous evening.

Her dinner with Russell had been an uncomplicated affair. He was easy to talk to and she had found, when he'd again asked about her men-friends, that she was telling him of Martin Walker. 'So I'm a bit off men just now—present company excepted,' she had told him with a smile, knowing instinctively that Russell felt the same as she—that they were friends and would never be, or want to be, more than that. She had an idea anyhow that he was still not over the woman whom he had once 'come close' to marrying.

They had dawdled over dinner and had dawdled over coffee, but at half past ten had stood in the hotel's car park about to part. Russell had said he was working in the north of England for the next few weeks, but would ring Aldwyn House on his return on the off-chance that she might be there.

'You never know,' she had answered lightly, and they had thanked each other for a pleasant evening, kissed cheeks, and he had stood in the car park and watched as she had driven away.

To her surprise the outside front porch light had been on when she'd reached Aldwyn House. She'd been surprised at Leon Beaumont's act of thoughtfulness. It had not been on when she had left. She had found she was smiling as she parked her car and went in.

Her temporary employer had not yet retired for the night. By his normal lifestyle she guessed that eleven o'clock at

65

night was early. She had noticed that the drawing room light was on. She had gone in. He had been reading, but had lowered his book to look at her, his eyes taking in the curve of a smile still on her mouth.

'You seem in good humour,' he remarked off-handedly.

Instantly Varnie was ready to rise. But, when never before had she bitten back some 'lippy' retort, she discovered, most weirdly, that she did not want to fight with him.

'You know how it is: good food, good wine, g—'

'Good company?' he finished for her—and she just had to burst out laughing. They might live in the same house, temporarily, but no way could they be said to enjoy each other's company.

'No offence,' she said.

'None taken,' he replied mildly, his eyes flicking from her laughing mouth to her sparkling eyes. 'You haven't imbibed too much, I hope?'

'With these bendy roads to contend with?' she asked. He almost smiled. Her heart gave the most idiotic hiccup. 'Er—can I get you anything—before I g-go up?' she enquired, feeling oddly breathless all at once.

'Thank you, no,' he replied, and she suddenly felt a need to get out of there and turned to leave the drawing room. 'Goodnight, Varnie,' he bade her quietly.

'Goodnight—Leon,' she managed, and went quickly.

She had not fallen asleep straight away. Had been awake for quite some while, her thoughts not on the man she had spent her evening with, but the man who had put the porch light on to guide her home.

Stuff and nonsense, she ridiculed herself now, springing out of bed. She went to have her shower, but had no clear idea of what she was 'stuff and nonsensing' about. Ridiculous!

Even more ridiculous, she found—and could not quite believe it, was that she was feeling most peculiarly shy about seeing Leon again. Shy? Honestly! She had never been shy! It must be the fact that they had been cooped up in the same house together for days on end.

Though when Varnie tried to analyse that thought she realized, since Leon was shut up in the study each day for hours at stretch, about the only time they were in each other's company for any prolonged length of time was when they breakfasted together. Which made the whole idea that she might feel shy with him just that—utter nonsense.

Utter nonsense or not, Varnie found that the only way to counter that shy feeling was to be as off-hand as he had appeared to be when she had first entered the drawing room last night.

As usual he was in the kitchen before her, and poured her a cup of coffee. 'Breakfast won't be long,' she said shortly. The kitchen was large; he seemed to fill it.

'I thought you hadn't drunk too much?' he answered, his tone equally short.

'I didn't!' she snapped.

'Then you're doing a fine impression of somebody badly hungover.'

She felt very much like asking how much he'd imbibed last night because he sounded much the same. But, perhaps aware the fault was hers, she swallowed the feeling and got on with grilling his bacon.

And so the day started, and so the week went on. For no reason she could think of she just could not be natural with him. And, to show how much it bothered him, he barely spoke to her.

Friday arrived—perhaps he'll go back to London for the weekend, or even permanently, she hoped. He did not. Saturday arrived. He was still there. Varnie wanted to ask him how much longer he was staying, but knew in advance she would get no sort of an answer. She left clean linen and towels outside his door and went shopping for fresh supplies.

On Sunday she decided to do something about the state

of the garden. True, everywhere was damp, and with the garden wearing its winter mantle it was never going to look its best. But she donned a thick sweater and trousers and set about raking leaves, and actually found she was enjoying herself.

An hour later, when Leon strolled out to watch her progress, she had a very tidy mountain of leaves piled up. 'Did I disturb you?' she asked, suddenly realising that the occasional clink of rake against stone—the garden seemed to grow stones—might have interfered with his concentration in the study.

He ignored the question, but surveyed the great heap of leaves she had just raked up. 'That lot will never burn,' he commented.

She did not care for his lofty attitude. She knew full well that she would never get a bonfire going with sodden leaves. So, in turn, she favoured him with a pitying look. 'I don't expect, as a mere townie, you have ever heard of a compost heap?' In actual fact to make a compost heap had not occurred to her until then.

Leon gave her a steady stare, then coolly remarked, 'You're back!' She eyed him warily. She had no idea what he was talking about. 'The lip,' he enlightened her.

'Lip?'

'Even your sauce is preferable to the mardy madam you've been for most of this week.'

'*Me*, mardy? That's rich! Anyone would think you'd got a mouthful of ulcers, the way you've been.'

His lips twitched. He controlled them. 'Pass me the rake,' he commanded, then ordered, 'And go and make some coffee.'

She stared at him and was aware, as her heart started to pound, that something fairly mammoth was happening to her that she did not want to happen. She felt breathless again, and thrust the rake at him. 'Do it properly!' she instructed, and went swiftly indoors.

By the time she reached the kitchen her world had righted itself and she knew just how absurd she was being. Mammoth? For goodness' sake! Nothing was happening to her other than she was stuck here with *him* and, because of Johnny, was likely to have to stay here with him until *he* decided he'd had enough of country air.

She had to admit, however, as her rebellion started to wane, that she was feeling a whole lot brighter suddenly. She made coffee and went out to tell Leon that coffee was ready with a smile, absent since Tuesday evening, playing around her mouth—Leon preferred her sauce to her mardiness?

Rounding the side of the house, Varnie watched the tall man in his good-quality shoes and trousers, shirt and light sweater who seemed to be enjoying his labours as she had. Back and forth went the garden rake.

'You've done this sort of thing before,' she accused when, as if aware he was being watched, he looked over his shoulder.

He stopped work. 'I can do with the exercise,' he replied, and she suddenly felt all soft inside about him; he'd been glued to his desk all week.

'Would you prefer your coffee out here or indoors?' she asked. 'I can bring it out if...' Her voice tailed away as a car halted at the bottom of the drive.

They both stared at it. Then, as the driver's door opened and its faintly familiar-looking occupant emerged, Varnie's sixth sense went to work. She looked swiftly to Leon. Oh, my word, thunder clouds! She might think she vaguely knew the man from somewhere—Leon *definitely* knew him.

Annoyance was all about Leon as he threw the rake from him and began to stride aggressively down towards the gate. Oh, grief! Recognition clicked. She had only seen the man once and that once, had been in a newspaper picture. He had been on the ground, holding his jaw—after Leon had thrown the punch that had floored him. The man was Neville

King and, by the way Leon was approaching the gate, Neville King was about to receive another one.

Instinctively, and without another thought, Varnie raced after Leon. She wasn't thinking. All she knew was that she did not want Leon to hit the man who believed he was his wife's lover—and nor did she want Neville King to hit Leon. Though there was little doubt in her mind who would come off second best.

'I take it your wife told you this address?' Leon did not bother with a greeting, his question tough and uncompromising as he reached down to unlatch the gates just as Varnie got there.

She blocked the gate-fastening with her body. And, for no reason other than if those gates were opened both men would be better placed to knock seven bells out of each other, she grabbed a hold of Leon's hand.

For her pains she was made to weather a look that said, What the hell do you think you're doing? But she was more concerned to prevent bloodshed than worried that Leon wasn't enamoured of her hand holding tactics.

'You must be Neville King,' she said brightly, smiling nicely at the newcomer and ignoring her glowering employer. Neville King did not look as if he would accept refreshment from the annoyed man her side of the gate, which gave her the courage to state, 'Leon and I were just about to have coffee. Would you like to join us?'

Neville King shook his head. 'No, thanks,' he replied civilly, and as she looked at him, looked into his face, she saw that he was a man who was dreadfully worn and tormented. She guessed it was not just the drive from London that was the cause for his weariness and torment. He was so in love with his wife, and Antonia King was, or had been, playing around with the man he had clearly come to North Wales to see. 'Toni told me last night that she was here last Tuesday,' Neville King turned to Leon Beaumont to state accusingly.

'So?' Leon challenged toughly.

'She said you were living here with your lady-friend. I've come to find out if it's true.'

'Mrs King didn't stay for coffee or tea either.' Varnie joined in the conversation hurriedly—plainly Neville King did not believe all the lies his wife told him. 'She was only here for a short while,' Varnie rushed on, feeling more than a touch desperate when Leon, while still looking clench-jawed at the other man, prised her hand away from his. It was his right hand. No way was she going to let that hand form a fist to once more flatten Antonia King's husband. 'In fact,' Varnie continued hastily, 'with Leon busy in the study, too busy to see anyone, I just had time to tell her— tell her…' Varnie started to falter '…our good news,' she brought out softly. Though, to be more exact, while her words might have been said softly they were said reluctantly, as far as she was concerned.

'You and…? You two are lovers?' Neville King asked bluntly. A non-permissible question, in Varnie's opinion— unless you looked into his unhappy, dejected sad eyes. The man was suffering, truly suffering. Never had she seen a man looking more tortured.

'That—' Leon began to clip—only to break off when Varnie galloped in, full pelt.

'Not that it's anybody's business but ours. Though—' she threw a sweet smile in Leon's nonresponsive direction '—I have to confess I'm—er—no stranger to Leon's bedroom.'

Leon turned. She wouldn't look at him, but she knew that he had his eyes on her and was probably staring at her as if she had just sprouted horns at the top on her head.

'How long has this been going on?' Neville wanted to know.

'Bloody cheek!' Leon barked, moving aggressively by her side, but all Varnie could think was that Neville must be anxious to know how long his wife's affair with Leon

Beaumont had been going on, and how long it had been ended.

'Quite some while,' she volunteered, and, hoping her grandfather would not mind in the circumstances—he'd had a terrific sense of humour, so he'd probably be laughing somewhere saintly, 'There has been a close bereavement in my family recently,' she explained rapidly. And, the words popping out of her mouth unsought, unthought—if she *had* thought she would never have said them, 'Because of that Leon and I have decided to postpone the announcement of our engagement out of respect for—'

'You're *engaged*!' Neville King's attention was all hers. 'You two are engaged?'

Oh, help—he'd kill her! 'Well, not officially.' She didn't seem able to stop. 'Out of respect, as I... But, yes, we're very definitely engaged.' She beamed. And, braving a glance to Leon's totally outraged expression, 'Leon did the bended knee bit—didn't you, darling?' she said. Unable to sustain looking at the glint of pure murder in his eyes, she moved her glance to the middle of his furious forehead. 'And I,' she ended simply, 'said yes.'

'I've had enough of this.' Leon almost drowned out the last bit, but Neville King had heard it, and actually seemed very much relieved—even as Leon thundered, 'If you've got anything to say, say it, and get off this property!'

'I've heard what I came to hear,' Neville King mumbled. But as he turned to go back to his car he smiled, actually smiled at Varnie.

And Varnie, turning away from the gate, didn't know whether to sprint back to the safety of the house or merely walk. 'That—um—coffee will be getting cold,' she commented on a strangled kind of note. She did not dare look at the man by her side, but knew that he was staring down at her. He said not one word. Ominous! Oh, Lord. 'It's getting a bit chilly,' she addressed the house in front of her.

Still nothing but that ominous silence. 'I think I'll—um—go in.'

She took off at a fast walk—Leon let her go. She did not trust that—she had an idea she was in big trouble. She remembered his fury when she had told him how she'd told Antonia King that they were live-in lovers. Oh, grief. He had called her conniving, as good as accused her of aligning herself with him for her own benefit, of broadcasting that they were lovers for her own ends... Oh, help, she was in big, *big* trouble.

Varnie made it to the house and made it to the kitchen. He did not follow. She hastily poured him a cup of coffee and, cowardly or not, made quickly for her room.

She knew he was mad, furious, and hoped it was all on account of Neville King daring to come to his sanctuary—daring to seek him out. Suddenly feeling far from cold, but feeling hot, hot, hot all over, she peeled off the heavy sweater she had donned for gardening and, tee-shirt-and-trousers-clad, raked distracted fingers through her hair. It was a foregone conclusion that she hadn't heard the last of this little episode, but perhaps if she did not see Leon again for a few hours it would give him time to cool down a little.

Varnie had just straightened her tee shirt when, to her horror, she heard the sound of footsteps on the stairs. Oh, heavens—he had not even waited to drink his coffee! She stood stock still, listening. Perhaps those footsteps would go on past her door.

They did not. They halted, right outside her door. She watched in fascinated dismay as the door handle turned. She swallowed, hard. Retribution was at hand.

Let him try. She might have skulked up here in the hope of his anger cooling down somewhat, but he would have hit that man, she knew he would, and Neville King had suffered enough. Now that it seemed it was her turn she did not intend to stand there and meekly take it.

Though she had to admit to feeling very much on shaky

ground when the door opened and, without so much as a by
your leave, Leon Beaumont came in. He was hostile, she
could see that he was. It was there in the lines of his body
and in the straight look in his eyes.

'Don't you ever knock?' she got in sharply first.

'What? At my fiancée's door?' As she had suspected, he
had not taken that well. Perhaps if she explained why she
had done it, why she had said what she had… Fat chance!
'I presumed, since you were no stranger to my bedroom,
that the same applied in reverse.' He was coming closer and,
not giving her the option to explain anything, was informing
her heavily, '*I* am *not* the marrying kind.'

'Well, of course. I—'

'Were I ever to lose my mind so completely as to even
think about taking such a drastic course, then trust me, *Miss
Sutton*, *you* would be the last bride I would choose.'

'As if I'd have you!' she retorted indignantly, then remembered that she was the one in the wrong here, and
backed down a trifle. 'Look, there's no need to get personal.
I only did what I did because—'

'You don't think to claim yourself as the future Mrs Leon
Beaumont might not be a touch personal?' he questioned
toughly. He came nearer. Varnie did not like it. She retreated a few steps.

'You were going to hit him,' she said in a hurry.

'What the devil has that got to do with you?' he asked
arrogantly.

'He looks beaten already. It's there in his eyes. He doesn't
need physical violence as well.'

'You don't know what you're talking about!' Leon
snarled shortly.

'I know you would have hit him. He would have hit you,'
she answered, stubbornly refusing to back down.

'I doubt it!' he rapped.

Varnie considered he had a point there. Should Leon have

landed him one, Neville King would in all probability have been too flattened to have the energy to hit back.

'That's not fair!' she erupted.

'What isn't?'

'It's too one-sided.'

'One-sided, hell!' Leon gritted. 'I've been put in a position here that I very much detest. I have tried to handle Neville King's paranoid jealousy tactfully. Tried to make him see that I have no interest in his wife whatsoever—God knows what far-fetched stories she spins him! I've been hassled by her, badgered by him—is it any wonder that I ran out of patience last week?'

'You knocked him down.'

'I'd had enough. And, for the record, he took a swing at me first.'

'Oh,' she mumbled. The press photographer hadn't caught that one. 'Well,' she defended, 'Neville King is only trying to save his marriage.'

'He hasn't got a marriage.'

'He hasn't?'

'You need to open your eyes too. His marriage is over—only he can't see it.'

'Over?' she echoed. 'Through you?'

Leon threw her an impatient look. 'Not through me! If it hadn't been me his wife set her sights on it would have been some other unsuspecting unfortunate.'

Varnie stared at him. He came closer yet. Close enough for her to see in his eyes that he hadn't yet started on sorting her out for what she had done. She moved to one side, nearer to the window. Leon halted, his grey eyes taking in her wary form.

Varnie knew then that she had to attack! 'Well, Antonia King isn't the only married woman you've—you've—er—had a liaison with,' was the best she could come up with.

Leon eyed her steadily for some moments. 'So you reck-

oned that by telling her that you and I were—what was it?—
live-in lovers, that I was madly in love with you, that—'

'You know why I said that,' Varnie interrupted quickly,
backing away again as he took a couple of steps that brought
him nearer still.

'For the same reason you've just told her husband that
you and I are engaged, no doubt,' he grated.

Oh, mother, he was much too close. Short of bolting from
her room—and pride would not allow that—she was running out of space to back into. 'No!' Pride kicked in right
there and then to demand that she stood her ground. 'You
know why I told Antonia King what I did!'

'Remind me. That was because…?' He came a step forward.

Her pride stayed high. She reckoned she had retreated
enough. 'If you remember, I was doing you a favour.'

'Favour!' he scoffed, and was right up to her, looking
down into her suddenly defiant wide sea-green eyes.

'Yes, favour!' she exploded. 'You wanted her out of your
hair—I settled it by telling her that you and I were…' she
started to falter '…well, you know.'

'And for the same reason—to get her husband out of my
hair—you told him we were engaged?'

'No. Not that. He was hurting. Is hurting. He needed re-
assuring that you and his wife aren't—er—carrying on behind his back. That's why he drove all this way down here
today. Because he wanted, needed, confirmation that what
his wife told him last night was true.'

'What a sensitive soul you are,' Leon Beaumont jeered.

Varnie recalled the pain she had witnessed in Neville
King's eyes. 'It's only natural to feel sensitive, sympathetic
to—' She began to defend herself—but was abruptly cut off
for her trouble.

'And what about *my* sensitivities?' Leon demanded, his
chin jutting aggressively.

'Wh…? How do you mean?'

'You know damn well how I feel about women. You know because I told you. Your first day here I told you.'

'I know, I know. There's no need to go on about it,' she bridled.

'Yet you deliberately set yourself up as my bed companion!'

'You know why!' She could feel herself going red.

'You deliberately invented emotions I'm supposed to have for you that are pure and utter fantasy.'

That stung. Quite clearly stalactites would become stalagmites before he even got to like her, let alone love her. 'You'll note I didn't lie about my feelings for *you*!' she erupted. 'At no stage did I invent that I was head over heels in love with *you*.' There was no need for him to know she had told Antonia King that they cared deeply for each other. 'My imagination just isn't that good!'

'Then you'll just have to pretend that it is!' he retorted angrily, his hands coming to her upper arms and holding her there.

She wasn't running. While admitting that she wasn't too happy that they were standing so close, almost toe to toe, she did not care too much either that until he took those firms hands from her she would not be able to run anywhere anyway—but she wasn't panicking. In all fairness perhaps she *had* rather overdone it by saying they were engaged.

'I suppose an apology isn't going to wash?' she offered.

'Too true it isn't,' he rapped. 'Antonia King has had since Tuesday to consider whether or not she wants my office, my directors, her fellow executives to know that I'm tucked away in a little Welsh love-nest. The fact that last night she told her husband about it indicates she has told everyone else.'

'Oh, surely not!' Varnie gasped, appalled. 'I didn't think of that wh—'

'Then you should have. As, too, you should have thought of the consequences before you blabbed to her husband that you and I are engaged. That snippet, if I'm not mistaken,' he said heavily, in the tone of a man who knew very well that he was *not* mistaken, 'will be all over the top floor come Monday.'

'No!' she gasped, and, swiftly, 'You can deny it. Nobody will take her word against yours.'

'If I was going to deny it I would have denied it the minute that ridiculous notion came out from your mouth,' he clipped.

'Why didn't you, then?' she rallied.

'For one, I couldn't believe my hearing! You, Varnie Sutton, have the cheek, the nerve, of old Nick. But, since I haven't denied I've popped the question that would see me tied to one woman for life—' he smiled a grim kind of humourless smile '—I don't see why I shouldn't take up the advantages you have just afforded me.'

Varnie stared at him, puzzled. 'I'm missing something here,' she had to admit. 'Just what are you saying?' she queried—and very nearly dropped when he told her.

'You have claimed we're lovers.' He shrugged. 'But for the life of me I cannot recall ever having had that—' he broke off to survey her figure '—pleasure. I suppose you could be thought quite fetching in that skimpy tee shirt...'

Varnie looked down to where her white tee shirt was clinging to her breasts—and alarm bells began to belatedly clamour. She gave a jerky tug to pull away from him. He held firmly on to her. He looked into her eyes, and seemed to enjoy the dawning look of alarm to be seen in them.

'I think I might as well have a sample now,' he commented, and began to draw her relentlessly up to him.

'No!' Varnie whispered, part of her still refusing to believe what was happening.

'Oh, but yes,' Leon mocked, his hold travelling to her shoulders.

She started to panic, started to feel desperate. 'I told you I was off men,' she hurriedly reminded him.

'It didn't do me much good telling you I was off women, did it?' he challenged, and instructed harshly, 'Get your mouth ready to receive, sweetheart.'

'You don't mean…' She found a stray strand of courage. 'Don't be ridiculous!' she ordered. 'Ooh…!' she exclaimed, and, as he hauled her into his arms and his mouth came over hers, she was unable to exclaim anything else.

His lips were warm against hers, and for a stunned moment she did not react at all. Then her body stiffened, unresponsive in his hold for a second, but a moment after that and she was pushing at him with all her strength.

'Don't!' she yelled at him when his lips left hers. 'Don't do this!' she ordered furiously.

'But why?' he mocked. 'You've claimed we're lovers. I should hate to think you're a liar.'

'Damn you…!' was as far as she got before his mouth once more claimed hers.

He pulled her close up against him, his mouth lingering over hers, stunning her with shock when she felt his hands on her back, on her bare skin under her tee shirt as he caressed and kissed her.

Again she jerked her head away. 'Don't!' she cried.

'Why not? I like the feel of your lovely silken skin.'

'You mustn't…' she tried, rather desperately.

'Oh, I think I must,' he drawled. 'How well I remember your nakedness, your beautiful body.' Oh, heavens! Her face burned at the memory of strolling into his bedroom that day with not a stitch on—all too obviously he had never forgotten it either. 'Surely, after all we have been together, you wouldn't deny me the right to touch that which I have only so far seen but not touched?'

She stared at him, her sea-green eyes huge in her face. 'No,' she whispered.

He smiled a smile she had no belief in. 'Darling,' he murmured, with about as much sincerity in that word as when she had used it on him, and his head came down once more.

Varnie wrenched her mouth away from his. She did not want him to kiss her, and wriggled wildly as she tried to break his grip. For the briefest of moments she thought she had twisted free, but she had only managed to twist round in his hold, and when she went to fly from the room it was to discover that she was going nowhere. Leon had caught her—her back was to him. And she knew when he held her there that he had not the smallest intention of letting her go.

'Where do you think you're running off to?' he taunted against her ear. 'We haven't finished yet.' He held her firmly against him and she felt the hardness of his body against her and she almost died when he placed his lips caressingly against the back of her neck, and breathed softly in her ear, 'In fact, sweetheart, we've barely started.' And then he stunned her into utter silence by moving his hands round to the front of her and unerringly cupping her breasts in his hands.

She gasped out loud. She had not even known he had undone her bra, but he had, effortlessly, and she felt the warmth of his palms moulding her full breasts, could feel his fingers as they teased at the hardened peaks.

She started to tremble and doubled over in an agitated bid to dislodge his hold. 'Don't!' she begged. 'Oh, please don't!' she cried, only to have her pleas ignored. He seemed to enjoy the feel of her breasts—she tried to get angry. 'Don't!' she yelled.

'That's better. I should hate you to be passive,' he jibed, and very near terrified her when, because she was small waisted and the waistband of her trousers gaped a little, he was able to transfer one of his hands inside the band of her trousers. He seemed to like the feel of her belly because, while she was still gasping at this new turn of events, both his hands were all at once inside her trousers, exploring.

She called out in alarm as his too intimate touch caressed

her warm belly. 'No!' she screamed, as his hands searched lower. 'No!' she implored again, in true alarm, and started not to merely tremble but to shake, the whole of her body visibly shuddering.

She knew the instant that her shaking had communicated itself to him, because Leon stilled in his intimate searching—and the next moment he had wrenched his hand from the inside of her trousers and, gripping her arms, had turned her to face him. There was no mockery in his expression as his eyes raked her face, as if to judge if she were play-acting.

Her white face told him that she was not, and he stared at her as if searching for words. Seconds, speechless seconds passed as he continued to stare into her white face. Then he drew a deep and controlling breath. 'I've—terrified you!' he managed at last, his words taut, sounding as if he could hardly believe what, in his anger with her for what she had done, he himself had done. 'It's all right,' he told her urgently. 'Shh.' He tried to calm her. 'You're all right. It's over. I won't harm you. I promise, you've nothing to fear from me.'

But Varnie was emotionally all over the place and wanted to be by herself. She pulled back from him. 'Go,' she said, her voice barely audible.

'You're shaking. You're…'

'I want you to go,' she repeated. 'I want you to go.'

He seemed torn about leaving her in the state she was in. 'You'll be all right on your own?' he asked, his eyes on her over-large wounded ones.

'I want to be by myself,' she insisted fixedly.

His hands fell to his sides, though for one most peculiar moment she had the feeling that he wanted to gently touch his lips to hers in a kiss of apology. His head did, in fact, come a fraction nearer. But, as if just then remembering how not many minutes ago he had half frightened the life out of her, he turned abruptly about and went striding from the room. As if to show that she was quite safe, he closed the door after him.

Varnie collapsed into a chair once he had gone, and gradually her shaking started to subside. She knew that what she should be doing was taking out her suitcase, packing and getting out of there. Surely even Johnny wouldn't expect her to stay after this?

But, strangely, something—she knew not what—seemed to be holding her back from taking that course of action. Most curiously, she found that she did not want to leave!

CHAPTER FIVE

How long she stayed sitting there she had no idea. But as she recovered from the shock of Leon's retribution for what she had done Varnie began to doubt that he would have taken her by force—had it got that far.

As far as he knew, though, she was a woman of some experience. Hadn't she after all answered yes when he had asked if she had slept with John Metcalfe? She had deliberately withheld the information that she and Johnny were family and that they had been small children at the time.

Leon still thought her a woman of some experience anyway, yet the moment he had realised that she was going into some kind of trauma from what he was about he had on the instant called a halt.

Varnie knew that, unless she intended to creep out of the house with her suitcase when he wasn't looking, she was going to have to face Leon again some time. But, using delaying tactics, she went and took a shower and changed into fresh trousers, shirt and light sweater. She had been dressed and ready for ten minutes, though, before she summoned up the nerve to leave her room.

She'd expected Leon to be at work in the study. He was not. When she was not at all ready to see him, and just as if he was expecting her first port of call would be the kitchen, he was there waiting for her when she went in. He was standing staring moodily out of the kitchen window, but turned about at the surprised sound of her 'Oh!'

'Don't worry,' he said gruffly, as if believing her cry had been from alarm rather than the surprise that it was. 'I won't be doing that again in a hurry.'

Varnie felt herself go scarlet as she recalled the warm

touch of his hands on her naked breasts and lower belly. Never had she known such intimacy. She pulled herself together. 'Can I have that in writing?' she asked waspishly. And, feeling choked all at once just from being in the same room with him, 'I'm going for a walk!' she announced stiffly.

'You're not leaving?' he questioned sharply.

'What—and deprive myself of your delightful company?'

He smiled. He actually smiled at her acid. 'And there was I thinking I might have irreparably damaged you. You're still smart in the mouth department, I see.'

She gave him a disgusted look and went out into the hall. She grabbed up her jacket from a peg by the rear door and took herself off.

Toad, she fumed as she trudged along, everything that had happened churning over and over in her head. She wanted to hate him for the fright he had given her. Yet how could she hate him? He had never intended his lovemaking—if you could call it that—to go very far. Just enough to pay her back, maybe.

Somehow on that walk—and she supposed she must have been out for a couple of hours—Varnie slowly came to the conclusion that, given the lies she had allowed Leon to believe with regard to her love-life and the experience he must have assumed that she had—she had got off more lightly than perhaps she deserved. She was dogged by an innate fairness that tripped her up to remind her that it couldn't be every day—or ever—that some female, without the least encouragement from him, piped up and claimed him as her fiancé.

So ask yourself, Varnie Sutton, did you suppose he would meekly sit back and say nothing? Did you expect to escape without some kind of censure, some kind of punishment? Particularly when you were aware that at this present time he had had his fill of women?

She supposed not.

It still didn't make what had gone on right, though. But as she returned to Aldwyn House, entering through the gates at the end of her walk, she found she had mellowed from being upset with him to being on the way to thinking that perhaps Leon was more sinned against than sinning.

And such way of thinking would never do, she told herself sternly. Had she forgotten that he was more or less blackmailing her to stay on? Yet, again, *was* he? She recalled how, up in her room, immediately after he had gone, she had somehow felt strangely reluctant to leave—and that had had nothing to do with her brother.

She recalled too, when she'd said she was going for a walk, how Leon had sharply questioned, 'You're not leaving?' Just as if he did not want her to go…

Well, of course he didn't want her to go. Who else would cook and clean for him if she wasn't there? Who would feed the brute? It was only his stomach he was thinking about.

Though as she entered the house she all at once realised that the brute had not been fed. She should have made him a sandwich over an hour ago! She went into the kitchen, mentally debating whether she felt forgiving enough to make him a snack, only to discover that she had no need to. He had made her one!

Feeling slightly stunned that in making his own sandwich he had made a sandwich for her too, Varnie experienced an overwhelming softening for him. He need not have. But he had. It was thoughtful of him, and it showed another facet of the man she was trying hard to hate, but who somehow she could not hate.

Weird, she decided. Perhaps his over-familiarity with her had tilted her world temporarily sideways? She decided there and then to stay out of his way until her world tilted the right way up again.

To stay out of his way proved surprisingly easy. She was in the habit of serving his dinner in the dining room.

Whether he thought that since their 'engagement' she might take it upon herself to eat there with him, she did not know, but he surfaced in the early evening and came to the kitchen to tell her coolly, 'I'll have dinner in the study.'

She nodded. If he wanted to work all night that was his business. 'Thanks for the sandwich,' she said, making her voice deliberately off-hand. As if she wanted to eat at the same dining room table, for goodness' sake!

Varnie went to bed that night feeling restless and totally out of tune with her world. She could not rid herself of the notion that as she wanted to keep her distance from Leon, so he too wanted to keep his distance from her. Well, it was working. She had hardly seen him! When she had gone to deliver his meal tray and then to collect his used dishes they had barely exchanged two words.

She was up early the next morning, with the notion pushing and pushing at her that Leon would probably be leaving any time now. Most peculiarly, that notion, that would at one time have seen her leaping with joy, strangely did nothing to lift her spirits that Monday.

She showered—used now to her shower throwing a temperamental fit halfway through—and dressed and went down to the kitchen, feeling a total mixture of unsettled emotions. Leon had scared her yesterday—and yet she couldn't think that it was the way he had come to her bedroom and all that had followed that was responsible for how she was feeling.

For once she was first in the kitchen, and she tried not to look at Leon when he came in for his first coffee of the day. She did not wish him good morning, and he did not appear to notice. But she found she had to look at him. He looks tired, she found herself thinking as, cup in hand, he went from the kitchen. And for no reason—because she was sure she didn't care if he worked every hour of every day on this, his 'holiday'—she discovered that she worried about him.

And that annoyed her. He was a grown man, for goodness' sake. If he wanted to spend his holiday working, that was up to him. Why on earth should that bother her?

But bother her it did. So much so that when, determined he was not going to have breakfast in his study too, she went and told him breakfast was ready, and he joined her in the kitchen, she found she was blurting out before she could stop it, 'You should get out more!'

He looked at her—silent, watching, maybe calculating why she thought anything that he did was anything to do with her. 'Jack's a dull boy?' he enquired, after long unsmiling moments of just looking at her.

She heartily wished she had kept her mouth shut. 'It's not good for you—working all the hours you do!' she said bluntly.

'This advice is all part of your skivvying service?' he enquired, equally bluntly.

Her face flamed. 'You can work till you drop for all I care!' she snapped, and, already having had enough of him—and the day had barely begun yet—she took herself off upstairs to do some tidying up.

She did hate him. But it did not last. By lunchtime she was again all out of tune, feeling very much mixed up—and rebellious. She had been here over a week now—ten days, in fact. And, while she was no stranger to hard work, and when the occasion demanded it no stranger to excessive work hours either, even skivvies—thank you, Beaumont, for the reminder—were allowed time off.

Afraid her feelings of mutiny might be as brief as her feelings of hate, Varnie took a sandwich in to him and, having had to wait a minute while he finished some business phone call, the moment he put down the phone she launched in with, 'I've decided not to cook tonight.'

He stared, unspeaking, at her. Clearly he was waiting for more. And at that moment she recalled how last night he had been at pains not to risk having to eat at the same table as her, and rebellion was joined by—devilment.

'Naturally I'd be lacking in my skivvying duties if I didn't make arrangements for you first.'

His eyes glinted with something. She knew not what. 'So?' Just that one clipped word and nothing else.

'So I can either take you for a meal—presumably I'm in for a handsome bonus at the end of your holiday,' she inserted, more from sauce than anything, 'or I can bring you back a takeaway.'

He opted for neither, but studied her as if wishing she would clear off and leave him to get on.

'Right!' Varnie exclaimed, rebellion high again. 'I'll bring you back a sweet and sour...' She paused, then added deliberately, 'Though not too heavy on the sour.'

The implication that he was sour enough was not lost on him. But, when Varnie was expecting her ears to be singed for her nerve, to her amazement she saw she had reached his sense of humour. He laughed. He actually laughed.

She stared at him, her heartbeats suddenly dancing a jig, her spirits all at once lightening. 'Without doubt, Varnie Sutton, you are the most impudent skivvy I have ever come across,' he informed her. Then, abruptly sobering, 'I wanted you to be certain that I pose no threat to you whatsoever,' he explained—and Varnie went all soft about him inside. This was why she had barely seen him?

'Because of—um—yesterday?'

He nodded. 'It was an unfortunate—incident. On reflection, I believe I overreacted somewhat, and I'm sorry about that.'

By the sound of it, he had plainly been playing all that had taken place yesterday over and over in his mind. 'Don't worry about it,' she said impulsively. 'No permanent harm done.'

He eyed her seriously. 'You're kinder than I deserve,'

he said shortly. But then asked, 'You feel—comfortable with me?'

'Of course,' she assured him.

He smiled a quiet kind of a smile, then, and she was glad to be friends once more—if they could ever have been termed 'friends' in the first place, which was very much in doubt. But, to her surprise, on that score she was more than a little shaken that, after a moment's thought, he should all at once decide, 'It seems to me, since you're determined not to cook tonight, that I'd better take you out to dinner.'

Instantly she was embarrassed. 'Oh, I wasn't angling for you to—'

'Do you think by now I don't know that?' he butted in.

And that pleased her. 'Er—right,' she mumbled.

Though, just to make sure she knew that it was nothing personal, 'As you observed—I should get out more,' he said.

Varnie dressed with care that evening. She told herself that she always dressed with care, and it had nothing to do with the fact that it was one Leon Beaumont who was to be her escort. Though for all the notice he took of her when, wearing a smart dress of a lovely shade of green that brought out the colour of her eyes, and with her long blonde hair about her shoulders, she went down the stairs, she might not have bothered.

'Ready?' was his only comment, and his glance barely skimmed her slender figure, curving beautifully in all the right places.

'As it's a Monday I didn't think there'd be any need for me to book a table anywhere,' she trotted out from an unthought nowhere. He might not have noticed that she was out of her usual trousers and top, but that did not stop her from noticing him. 'Most eating establishments are quiet on a Monday,' she heard herself rattling on. My word, was he handsome. She had only ever seen him in casual clothes, but suited, with collar and tie, he was something else again.

'At least—' she didn't seem able to stop babbling on '—that's my experience of the hotel trade.'

He could have told her to shut up, that she was giving him earache before the evening began. But he didn't. Though he succeeded in surprising her into speechlessness anyway when he affably informed her, 'I've booked.'

He had earlier taken his car out from the garage and parked it on the drive, and they were out of the house and getting into the car before Varnie was over her surprise. 'You've booked? You don't know anywhere!'

He turned in his seat, favoured her with a superior look and, turning back to start up his long, dark and sleek vehicle, instructed, 'It's your night off—try to enjoy it.'

It was not difficult to enjoy it. Varnie was thrilled and delighted that the establishment Leon had chosen for them to dine on her night off was the splendid Ruthin Castle. Parts of the castle, now a hotel, dated back to the thirteenth century. It was set in acres and acres of gardens and parklands, and yet still managed to be close to the medieval town of Ruthin, a centuries-old town that in 1400 had been attacked by the army of the Welsh chieftan *Owain Glendower*. It was a joy to Varnie to walk with Leon into the wood-panelled reception, and to go on to sit with him in a lounge area with a pre-dinner drink.

She did not know what she had expected but, had she nursed any thoughts that the evening would be spent in some sort of spasmodic monosyllabic conversation, she discovered she could not have been more wrong. Johnny had said that Leon had charm by the bucketload. And he had. She sipped her drink and was amazed by how the evening was going! Leon charmed her by inviting her opinion on any subject that came up, and, more, with never a cross word between them, genially allowed her opinion when it did not exactly match his own.

She was having a really pleasurable evening, she realised, and wondered if her pleasure stemmed from the fact that she had usually been too busy at the business end of hotel life to be able to just sit back and relax. Or could it just be the company she was with? That thought startled her, and she jerked a glance to Leon.

'Was it something I said?' he asked, amusement playing at the corners of his mouth.

She shook her head. 'I've just realised I *am* enjoying myself.'

'You didn't expect to?'

'Well…' she prevaricated, for in truth she was feeling a little mixed up inside.

'Well?' he prompted.

'We—er—didn't get off to a very good start, did we?'

'You were lippy,' he documented.

'And you were as suspicious as the devil,' she said lightly, a touch stunned that they were getting on so well. Though as a mixture of guilt smote her, about the way she was deceiving him by not telling him that she was John Metcalfe's sister, and was joined by the memory of her nerve in telling both Antonia King and her husband what she had, so Varnie saw that this could only be a short respite between her and Leon. 'And tomorrow you'll be back to the suspicious devil I met ten days ago.'

'And tomorrow you'll go back to being a pert baggage without a care to what lies you tell complete strangers.'

That was too close to home, and although she knew he was referring to the lies she had told the King duo, Varnie's conscience was again tweaked with regard to her lies of omission in connection with her brother. 'Truce?' she pleaded. 'If I promise to do my best not to be lippy again, not to tell any more lies, and you promise to try not to return to being a grumpy brute—' She broke off when it looked as if he would accuse her of being lippy again already. Varnie gave him her best grin, and he seemed fascinated for a few moments by her mouth, and she went on, 'Shall we call a truce—just for tonight?'

He considered the matter. 'That shouldn't be too difficult,' he agreed. And Varnie laughed out loud when, simultaneously, they both touched wood. It was his turn to grin—and Varnie was on the way to thinking that there must be something quite magical in the air around Ruthin Castle.

Indeed, everything about the evening seemed to have been touched with magic. They were still talking, not rowing, when they were shown to their table in the dining room. In fact, so in tune did they seem to be, they had both ordered the delicious sounding glazed goat's cheese on a tomato and shallot salad with a port wine dressing for a starter.

They were on their main course when, apropos of absolutely nothing, although her eyes were alight—she was finding him a most stimulating dinner partner—quite out of the blue he looked across at her and, totally involuntarily, she was sure, suddenly said, 'You really are exquisitely beautiful, Varnie.'

Then he abruptly looked away, just as if cursing because his unthought comment—in view of past history—may have made her feel uncomfortable with him. What was a girl to do? 'I wondered when you'd notice,' she said, a cheeky grin on her face so he should know that she had not wondered at all. But, as well as seeming a touch relieved that he had not completely ruined the atmosphere between them, Leon looked a little surprised too at her answer, and she found she was going on, 'I come downstairs in my best frock— having changed out of my skivvying outfit—and all you can say is, "Ready?".'

Suddenly she wished she had not said that last bit. She was making this much too personal. And that was not what this evening was about. What this evening was about, she only then realised, was the two of them getting back to the way they had been before Leon had come to her room yesterday and begun kissing her.

'I'm sorry,' she apologised. 'I'm making this much too personal, and it isn't about that, is it?'

He did not answer her question, but documented, 'With the best will in the world, bearing in mind we're neither of us machines, I'd say, since we are in daily contact, that it would be surprising if "personal" did not creep into it now and then.'

She thought about that, but only for a moment. 'You're right, of course,' she realised. 'I hadn't analysed it that way....' Her voice tailed off. Did he think about her when she wasn't there—the way she did of him? No, said the brighter part of her brain. Not that she wanted him to, insisted another part of her, the proud part.

'But since we are being a touch personal...'

'Are we?'

'I've decided we are.' He smiled to take any hint of bossiness out of his statement. 'Just for this evening.' And, while her heart gave the most peculiar flutter, 'Now, tell me about Varnie Sutton.'

No way! Everything in her backed away in alarm. For herself, her life was an open book. But she was Johnny's sister, and Johnny's job—the job he loved; she mustn't forget that—was at risk here.

'You know all there is to know,' she answered lightly.

Leon looked at her sceptically. 'I thought you weren't going to tell any lies tonight,' he said accusingly.

'When did I promise that?' she exclaimed in mock alarm. Quickly she turned the conversation to him. 'How about you? Tell me about you?' she invited.

He gave her a wry look, but enquired, 'Where would you like me to start?'

At the very beginning. Suddenly Varnie found she felt curious to know all that there was to know about him. 'Well—er—in order to spare my blushes, I suppose you'd better give me the edited highlights only,' she suggested.

'You weren't going to be saucy either,' he reminded her.

She laughed; she was having a splendid time. 'Well, and it's true. I expect, you do have—um—a bit of a reputation.'

He seemed genuinely a shade surprised. 'In what area?' he wanted to know.

Surely he already knew? 'With—the ladies.' She immediately apologised. ':I'm sorry, I shouldn't have said that. But you did decide to be "a touch personal".'

'Wretched woman,' he called her lightly, and Varnie fell just a little in love with him. Nonsense, objected her head. 'You're referring to Antonia King?' Leon enquired.

'She's just one of many, I suspect,' Varnie replied, feeling oddly a touch *eau de nil* around the gills. 'Weren't you recently involved in some rather unsavoury divorce?'

Leon looked at her levelly for some seconds, but, when Varnie would not have been at all surprised had he curtly told her to mind her own damn business, he merely shrugged. 'They were separated,' he answered. 'The lady in question was living apart from her husband well before I arrived on the scene. I only took her out a couple of times anyway—we'd stopped seeing each other before said husband attempted to involve me as a reason for not paying up when she decided on a divorce and tried to relieve him of a fortune he wasn't keen to part with.' Leon shrugged again. 'My lawyers eventually saw them both off.'

'You came out the innocent party?'

'I sure as hell had nothing to feel guilty about. Though mud clings, if only briefly.'

She supposed that it did. Though even the most ghastly happenings were only nine-day wonders before the next news item arrived. 'And then there was Antonia King. You were innocent there too?'

'Even less guilty there. I never so much as thought of the woman in any way other than as a valued member of the team. I should have dismissed her the moment she started to come on to me.'

'Why didn't you?' she enquired, interested.

Leon gave self-deprecating look. 'Pride, I suppose. It seemed more than a mite feeble, from where I was looking at it, that I should get rid of the woman solely because she was—hmm—after me.'

He was embarrassed! Varnie laughed softly. 'No wonder you're fed up with women—two in general, one in particular,' she itemised. 'So fed up you decided it was time to get away from the lot of them. That it was time to take a holiday.'

'And barely had I closed my eyes in my isolated retreat,' Leon took up, his eyes steady on her face, his small embarrassment gone, 'than, as naked as the day you were born, you walk in.'

Her skin burned. 'Don't remind me!' She was the one to be embarrassed now.

'Perhaps that was a little unfair,' he conceded with a gentle kind of smile. 'You're blushing.'

'I *know*!' she exclaimed huffily.

And he grinned, totally unoffended by her sharp tone. 'Your turn,' he said.

'My turn?'

'Aw, come on. It's not every day, or ever, that I share such confidences over dinner. You're obliged, out of courtesy if nothing else, to share a confidence with me.'

She thought she could argue that statement, but instead asked, 'Such as?'

'Such as—the man you dumped when you found out he was married.'

'Martin!' she said with a start of surprise. Only ten days ago she had thought she loved Martin. Now she could not recall the last time she had thought of him.

'You were in love with him?'

She shook her head. She knew now that she had never been in love with Martin. 'I thought I loved him. I was going to go on holiday with him, but when he was late meeting me at the airport I rang his office and learned he was married and that he had children.'

'There was no mistake? About him being married?'

Varnie shook her head. 'His secretary said his wife had been at his office with the children only that day. Besides, I asked him. As soon as he turned up at the airport, I asked him.'

'He admitted it?'

'Reluctantly, I think. He said he hadn't seen his wife in ages, and that they were getting divorced.'

Varnie looked across at Leon. He had an understanding kind of look in his eyes. 'Poor Varnie,' he said softly. But, his tone sharpening, 'You're better off out of that sort of relationship.'

She looked down, and was a little staggered to see that they had eaten their way through the main course with her barely noticing. But, when she might have commented on it, the notion was taken completely out of her head by Leon's next remark, and she looked up again, sharply.

'I suppose it *was* a full-blown relationship?' he asked point-blank.

His nerve was staggering! 'If by full blown you mean did I sleep with him,' she replied snappily, 'then it is absolutely none of your business.'

Leon eyed her steadily for several moments, and then declared, 'You didn't.'

She had to laugh. He was a most infuriating man, but, yes, he made her laugh at the oddest moments. 'That was delicious,' she said, casting her eyes to her cleaned plate.

They had been served their last course when Varnie began to feel a tinge of regret that this magical evening was almost over. She guessed it would not be repeated. Holidays, even working holidays, had to end some time, and while she still had no idea when Leon intended to leave, she felt instinctively that the call of his office would soon get to him. Soon he would leave—this evening would be a one-off and would never happen again.

She looked across at him—only to find Leon had stopped eating, as if arrested by some sudden thought. 'What?' she asked. And, when he did not immediately answer but continued to look at her, a touch speculatively, she felt, 'I've got cream on my chin?'

His mouth quirked upwards at the corners. 'Your chin is delightfully cream-free,' he replied, but did not shrink from asking about that which he did not know. 'In relation to your non-relationship with the contemptible married Martin, just how experienced are you, Varnie?'

She stared at him, totally taken aback. 'What has that got to do with the price of firelighters?' was the best she could come up with at such short notice. He was not put off.

'You yesterday told Neville King that you were no stranger to my bedroom, allowing him to swallow the obvious implication. But you and I both know the truth behind your familiarity with my bedroom, don't we?'

'I'm—er—not comfortable with this conversation,' Varnie retorted primly.

'Well, we can't have that!' Leon said toughly, and she hated him that he had brought a sour note into her magical evening. 'As I remember it, I had to put up with a conversation where, astonishingly, when you knew full well how I feel about women just now, you claimed to be engaged to me.'

'Don't be stuffy!'

'Stuffy? Your nerve is astounding!' he accused curtly.

'Well, yours isn't so dusty!' she retorted. 'I've kept out of your bedroom—it's a pity you didn't keep out of mine!' Immediately the words were out, she regretted them. 'I'm sorry,' she apologised at once. 'I'm so sorry. You're feeling badly enough about that without me rubbing it in. Forgive me,' she said, and looked across at him—to see that all at once every scrap of aggressiveness had gone from him.

'Me, forgive you?' he asked quietly. 'You really are quite a lovely lady.'

Her heart started to thunder at the gentle look in his eyes, at the compliment he had just paid her. She shook her head. 'I'm lippy, and I tell lies,' she reminded him.

'Both, regrettably, true,' he agreed. But, proving as she was discovering that when he was on the trail of something he never let up, 'So, neither lippy or lying this evening—your other lover, so you led me to believe, was John Metcalfe. Want to tell me about him?'

Most definitely not. She shook her head. 'Some things are private,' she replied flatly. He looked at her long and hard, but did not look likely to give up. 'And you're on the way to ruining what had been a very pleasant evening,' she told him quietly. He seemed to bend a little. She smiled sweetly. 'And it has to last me—I've got this tyrant of an employer who seldom lets me have a night off,' she informed him.

He laughed, seeming unable to prevent himself from laughing at her sauce. He shook his head. 'My stars, the man who eventually gets you is going to have to keep on his toes.'

She laughed too. 'He'll be special,' she said.

'He'll need to be.'

They had coffee, but when Leon called for the bill Varnie remembered that she had initially said that she would take him out to dinner. 'I'll settle it,' she told him.

'I'll deduct it from your bonus,' he replied, straight-faced. She looked into his eyes—his eyes were smiling.

The magic had returned as they walked from the castle to where Leon had parked his car, and Varnie knew, without analysing the why or how of it, that the evening had been a 'bonus' kind of an evening. She hadn't expected it to be when she had thrown that 'I can take you for a meal' option at him. Or expected it when he had turned the tables on her and said, 'I'd better take you out to dinner.'

Seated beside him as Leon drove them back to Aldwyn House, she was silent as she reflected that the evening had been a one-off. Tomorrow there was every possibility that he would go back to being grumpy—though just then she did not want to remember Leon as being bad-tempered with her—and she in all probability would go back to being impudent; though she sincerely hoped she wouldn't be called upon to tell any more lies, either directly or by omission.

With Leon busy with his own thoughts, as well as concentrating on his driving, Varnie relived the pleasantness they had shared. Unbelievable, really, when she thought of how instantly they could be at each other's throats. She recalled his charm, the numerous topics they had chatted over, his easy way when she'd occasionally had an opinion that was at odds with his own. Though they had not differed too often, she all at once realised. In fact, they seemed to think alike about a lot of matters.

He had trusted her with his confidences too, and she really felt good about that. She remembered how she had—unforgivably, in her view, and so carelessly—well, okay, she had been cross at the time—reminded him of that episode in her bedroom. She had not really needed to remind him. He'd already been giving himself a hard enough time over that, without her sourly reminding him.

They arrived at Aldwyn House, and as Leon got out of the car to go back and close the gates they had just driven in through, so Varnie was overwhelmed with remorse, and a feeling that, as Leon had trusted her, she wanted to let him know that she trusted him.

She had no idea at all how that could be achieved. It was not until they were standing in the hall, the house locked up for the night, when Leon said, 'Thank you for a very pleasant evening, Varnie,' and she looked up into his eyes, that the answer came to her.

She moved that yard or so closer. 'Thank you, Leon, I really enjoyed it,' she said with a smile, and, so natural did it feel just then, she moved another step nearer, placed her hands on his shoulders, and stretched up and kissed him.

It was a warm, trusting, not passionate, but unhurried kiss. She felt his mouth move against hers, and for a moment she thought he was going to respond. But the only response he made was not to take her in his arms but to take hold of her arms—as though to hold her off, as though to push her away!

She stepped back, felt a rush of colour flare to her face. 'You'd—um—better deduct that from my bonus too,' she said chokily—and turned smartly about and, trying not to run, went swiftly up the stairs.

CHAPTER SIX

NEVER, ever could Varnie recall feeling so embarrassed. That kiss, that unwanted kiss she had bestowed on Leon, haunted her through her waking hours that night. And, because she slept only fitfully, her waking hours were many.

She just did not know how on earth she was going to face him again, and was up out of her bed early, beating down the instinct to leave right now and thereby obviate any need to see him again at all.

Against that were thoughts of her brother. But so discomforted did she feel that she was strongly torn to let Johnny go hang.

She sighed as she recalled how, apart from his initial reaction, Leon had frozen when she had kissed him. Oh, heavens!

Varnie looked at her suitcase, but thoughts of Johnny, for all her inclination to let him go hang, would not let her take what seemed the only answer. How could she go now that her capricious brother had found and wanted to keep the job he said he had always been searching for?

She sighed again as she realised she would have to stay and would have to keep up the pretence that she was an ex-girlfriend of Johnny's. Having got to know Leon a little, she had an idea he would hit the roof if he knew the truth and that, since the house belonged to her, he was beholden to her.

Yet, maybe from her innate honesty, she felt she wanted to be open with Leon—only Johnny's job, she knew, would be well and truly on the line were she to tell Leon. Add to that the fact that Leon did not like favours, and took them from no one, and it was plain to her that any confession from her would ensure that there would be nothing for her changeable brother to return from Australia for.

All of which, Varnie knew as she dithered about leaving her room, was doing absolutely nothing to get her through the awkwardness of seeing Leon again. It was not as if she went around forwardly kissing, without sign of invitation, every man she had dinner with.

She left her room and went down the stairs, realising that in her attempt to let Leon see that she fully trusted him she had only made a bad situation worse. Should she try to explain that her action had only been to let him know that she trusted him?

Perhaps he had seen that anyway, she pondered as she crossed the hall into the kitchen. With relief she saw that she was first down again. Her relief was short lived when just then the most awful thought struck her. She all at once recalled how Leon had said that Antonia King was more interested in his wallet than him. And last night he had intimated that that woman he had taken out a few times had been after a huge divorce settlement from her husband.

Oh, my heavens. Varnie blanched. Was Leon now revising his opinion about her. Did he now think that she was another female on the make? Oh, she could not bear it if he did.

Such thoughts occupied her for the next worrisome ten minutes as she prepared his breakfast. At the end of those ten minutes, though, her pride appeared and was on the march, so that the embarrassment that had kept her sleepless through the night was in hiding when a sound behind her alerted her to the fact that she had company. She spun about.

'I'm not after your money!' she erupted.

Leon stood and surveyed her mutinous expression before drawling easily, 'That's still the last time I'm taking you out to dinner.'

She coloured up, could feel herself going scarlet. 'I meant me k-kissing you last night,' she said shortly.

'And I meant if you're this bad tempered after a night out, it might be better if you stayed in.'

'Mmp!' She sniffed. 'That kiss…' she tried.

'If you're thinking of kissing me again—don't!'

'I wouldn't kiss you again if—' she began hotly.

'Good,' he cut in, adding—though not to make her feel any better, she felt sure, 'So now we're quits.'

'Quits? You kissed me more than once,' she reminded him, stormily. 'And—' She broke off. Even her ears felt on fire as she just then recalled his hands on her breasts, his hands on her skin. 'Quits,' she snapped. 'Good.' And, putting his breakfast to keep warm until he was ready for it, she went speedily from the kitchen. He could see to his own coffee. Never had she known such a man for so upsetting her equilibrium.

Varnie collected the vacuum cleaner and other cleaning equipment and set to work. She did not particularly want to consider the brute, but if he had work to do that called for any degree of concentration it would be better if the vacuuming was done before he got started.

She later took the cleaner upstairs and recalled how previously she would have dearly liked to go to Leon's room and give it the once-over. But she managed to keep her housekeeping instincts in check, and apart from leaving fresh bed-linen and towels outside his door she left him to fend for himself.

That morning he could wallow in dust and fluff until it was up around his ears before she would dream of flicking a duster over his room.

She was still in a mutinous frame of mind—who did he think he was, telling her not to kiss him again?—when she decided that she needed to get out, be it only as far as the nearest supermarket.

Varnie was undecided how long she would be away, and knew that but for Johnny she would not be coming back. She made a sandwich for Beaumont, and, most definitely out of sorts where he was concerned, would have liked to substitute something toxic instead of mustard. She wrapped his sandwich in a napkin and put it where he would find it, then took herself off to the shops.

Varnie began to feel better for being away from Aldwyn House. And yet, bizarrely, she had the extraordinary feeling of a kind of homesickness, a sort of feeling as if she wanted to be back there. As if she wanted to be back there with Leon, as if her home was there—with him.

Bizarre wasn't the word for it! She decided that the strain of living incarcerated with the brute must be getting to her. She deliberately made herself have lunch out. Though when the compulsion to be back at Aldwyn House became too much for her to ignore she opted to have neither pudding nor coffee. Had she known what awaited her when she got back, she later thought, she would have stayed out to tea as well.

She found she was singing softly to herself on the journey back. Proof, if proof she needed, that her outing had done her good. When moodiness was not a part of her nature, she had felt in a very dark mood on her way out.

She was surprised to see a car standing in the drive when she reached the house. It was a car she did not recognise and belonged to neither of their recent visitors.

Since she was not expecting anyone to make a call, Varnie could only suppose it must be some friend or business acquaintance Leon had invited. Feel free! She felt her equilibrium start to tilt once more, and decided that, whoever it was, she did not want to know. She would put her bits of shopping away and either stay in the kitchen until they had gone or go up to her room.

So much for that idea! Barely had she got in through the rear door than Leon was coming from the drawing room and along the hall. She flicked a glance to him, and was undecided if some brief nod of her head would do by way of saying, Hello, I'm back, when, to her absolute and utter astonishment, 'Darling,' he greeted her—for all the world as if he had truly missed her. 'Let me take that shopping for you.'

Varnie blinked, and was thinking of having her hearing checked the next time she saw a doctor. 'What?' she queried faintly. But as Leon came forward and took the plastic carriers from her, so she spotted the man and woman who had followed him from the drawing room.

'I'll just drop these in the kitchen,' Leon commented generally, but was so quickly back that Varnie had no time to do more than look at the other two. He straight away introduced the three of them, if briefly, then stated pleasantly, 'Pauline and Eddie were just leaving.' And, with a warm smile to Varnie, he proceeded to explain, 'Our secret's out, I'm afraid.'

Varnie had not the smallest idea what he was talking about. 'Oh?' she queried, every antenna on the alert to tell her it was not only in the woodshed that there was something nasty.

'Leon tells us that the two of you met when he stayed overnight in the hotel where you were employed,' Pauline remarked.

That was how she had told him she had met Johnny! Varnie could only thank her years of hotel training that she managed to keep her face straight. Presumably there was a point to what Leon had told his two friends.

'Is it any wonder I decided to stay an extra night at that hotel?' Leon went on, shaking Varnie rigid by placing an arm familiarly about her shoulders.

'No wonder at all,' Eddie said appreciatively.

'I'm sorry about your loss,' Pauline addressed Varnie as the four of them edged to the front door.

Had thieves broken in while she had been out? 'I explained about your close relative,' Leon informed Varnie. It explained nothing as far she was concerned.

'It—was—er...' she began to mumble.

'Forgive us,' Leon butted in. 'It's still very painful for Varnie.'

'Of course,' Eddie said sympathetically.

Leon opened the front door and, with his arm still about Varnie, he ushered Pauline and Eddie out to their car.

Varnie was very inclined to shake Leon's arm away. She owned that being tucked into his side like that was making her feel all funny inside. But for some odd reason, feeling a loyalty to him that she was sure he did not deserve, she let his arm stay.

The moment the car Eddie and Pauline had come in was driven out of sight, however, and Varnie pulled vigorously away. More vigorously than she'd needed to, it seemed, because Leon was quite as keen to immediately let go of her, and she almost lost her balance.

There was no 'almost' about her temper, though; that was well and truly lost. 'What the Dickens was that all about?' she exploded.

Leon looked down at her from his lofty height and, not a bit abashed, quite casually drawled, 'You wanna be my fiancée, you'll have to put up with it when the press come to call.'

'W... B... P...' Witlessly, her sea-green eyes wide, Varnie stared at him. 'They—Eddie and Pauline—they aren't your friends?' she gasped. And, as more brain power managed to surface over shock, 'You told them we were *engaged*!' she squeaked.

He shook his head. 'You did that yourself!' he reminded her bluntly.

'No, I di... When did I?' she demanded.

'Shall we go in?' Leon enquired, a quiet kind of phoney pleasantness in his voice.

She did not want to go in. She was good and mad, and wanted to sort this out right here and now. But Leon was leaving her standing there with no one to argue with—and only then did she notice that it had started to rain.

She followed him into the drawing room. 'When did I?' She kept up the attack. 'I'd never even met them before, so how could I possibly have told them that I was engaged to you?'

'You made news of our engagement press copy on Sunday, when you announced to Neville King that we were very definitely engaged. That I had done the "bended knee" bit,' Leon retorted.

Varnie looked at him open-mouthed. 'You called the press in?'

'Would I?' he questioned toughly.

'Neville King?'

'Either him or his wife. Whatever—my office will have that little titbit by now.'

Oh, my hat! He had suspected it would be all over the top floor by yesterday. She felt faint. 'Eddie and Pauline—they're press reporters?' she rallied to question that which she now saw was pretty obvious.

'Pauline's the reporter. Eddie's a photographer.'

'Photographer! You didn't let him take—?'

'Eddie was keen to have a photograph of the two of us together,' Leon cut in shortly. 'I borrowed your "close family bereavement" tale and told him I would not sanction any photograph of you being used.'

Varnie was touchy about that 'close family bereavement', even if it had been she who had started it. 'Why didn't you deny it?' she charged crossly.

'What—and make you a liar?' he mocked.

She felt a terrible urge to hit him. She managed to hold it down. 'It's not funny!' she exploded.

'You should have thought of that on Sunday!' Leon rapped. 'You were the one who started the rumour.'

'But you needn't have gone along with it!' she returned hotly.

He smiled. It was a smile too silky to be trustworthy. 'True,' he replied nicely. 'But, on thinking about it, to be engaged to you for a short while seems a small price to pay for a spot of relief from women who won't take no for an answer.'

Varnie threw him a disgusted look. She had got herself into this, and she knew it. 'I hope your ferrets drown!' she hurled at him, and marched out of there along the hall and to the stairs.

She was halfway up the stairs when Leon came out into the hall. She was at the top of the stairs when his voice floated up to her. 'Do I take it I'm making my own dinner?'

She did not answer, but carried on to her room, her lips twitching. Hate him she might, but he still had the power to make her laugh. It was too late to wish she had not purchased his choice of newspaper for him while she was out.

Varnie went down the stairs a short while later to put the shopping away. She supposed she would make dinner for him, and supposed too that one crisis cancelled out another. First thing that morning she had been embarrassed to death to face Leon after kissing him so last night—while not a passionate kiss, it had been no mere peck either. But since coming back from shopping she had not given it another thought. Other priorities had taken over.

She peeled potatoes and dwelt on her 'engagement'. While it was plain that it fell into the 'nine-day wonder' category, if it lasted that long, she supposed she had better try and accept—since she was the one who was guilty of starting the 'engagement' ball rolling in the first place, that for the rest of Leon Beaumont's stay at Aldwyn House they were engaged.

She could not say that she liked it. But could not see that she was in any position to do anything about it. Eddie and Pauline had found them and... Oh, heavens. Another thought hopped into her brain and, without stopping to think, Varnie hurriedly left the kitchen.

'I knew you were mad at me,' Leon drawled as she

slammed into the study, 'but do you really want to set about me with that lethal-looking instrument?'

Varnie looked to where he was looking—so urgent was her business she still had the potato peeler in her hand. 'If those two press people found you, what's to prevent other newshounds coming down here?'

'You flatter me.'

'You *exasperate* me!' she snapped. His lips twitched. Oh, to be able to box his ears! 'You're well known. There'll be hordes of press people descending…'

'Hordes?' he echoed. 'I doubt I'm that well known. But,' he went on, when she would have jumped in to contradict him, 'I let that pair believe that you were out shopping for a few things you needed to take with us when we leave later this afternoon.'

'You told then we were leaving?'

'For a more private location. I rang my PA a short while ago and told her to make sure the news that you and I are leaving Wales in a few hours reaches Antonia King's ears today.'

'You think of everything!' Varnie said shortly, and marched back to the kitchen. He patently considered that if any of the newspaper people questioned the veracity of what Eddie or Pauline might pass on, then either Antonia King or her husband would confirm it.

Varnie did not see anything of Leon for a few hours, but knew when he had left the study and when he went to the drawing room. Knew when he left the drawing room and knew when he went to take his shower. She was busy putting the finishing touches to an apple pie when he joined her in the kitchen.

'Is that for us?' he asked, leaning negligently against a dresser. She gave him a look, as if to ask whom the devil he thought she was making it for. As if reading her thoughts, he quirked his lips. And after a second or two he commented, 'It seems ridiculous that you eat in here and I take dinner in the dining room. You may as well lay another place in the dining room,' he decided.

He was inviting her to eat her meal with him? Magnanimous! An imp of mischief she seemed unable to suppress all at once jumped into the fray. And though that very morning Varnie had been so embarrassed that nothing would have seen her referring to the way she had parted from him the previous evening, the afternoon's happenings seemed to have sent all embarrassment on its way. She enquired nicely, 'You're—um—not afraid of the consequences after dinner?' her eyes wide and innocent.

Leon looked at her, looked into her saucy innocent eyes. And Varnie knew from the suddenly laid-back look of him that there was nothing wrong with his recall. That he had no difficulty at all in remembering the way she had taken it upon herself to kiss him when they'd returned to Aldwyn House.

He smiled a nice if phoney smile. 'You're worried, post-apple pie, that you might not be able to control your—sexual urges?' he replied delightfully.

Sexual urges! Now she *was* embarrassed. There had been nothing remotely sexual in the way she had last night kissed him. Had there? She was suddenly too hot and bothered to know. But, although she felt a touch pink around the ears, she managed to stay outwardly calm, at any rate, to scoff, 'You think I might be unable to resist throwing myself at you?'

He shrugged, and smiled a silky smile. 'It has been known,' he informed her.

Pig! She hadn't thrown herself at him! But that was what he was intimating; she knew full well it was. And what could she do about it? Nothing. 'You'll forgive me, I'm sure—' she favoured him with a phoney smile of her own '—but if it's all the same to you I'll decline your most generous offer.'

Her sarcasm did not so much as put a pinhole in him.

And she had to admit he looked far from broken-hearted as he stood away from the dresser and politely told her, 'Suit yourself,' prior to ambling casually out of the kitchen.

The words 'sexual urges' haunted Varnie for the remainder of that day, and she was still thinking of Leon's accusation when she lay in her bed, trying to get to sleep that night.

She was sure that she hadn't 'come on to him' in that sense. Yet somehow there was a stray niggle of doubt. Varnie thumped her pillow and tried to get to sleep—had she kissed him a little longer than she should? Had that 'I trust you' kiss turned into an 'I wouldn't mind a bit more response' type of kiss?

No, no, no, she denied. And made up her mind there and then that for however much longer she was going to have to stay here—my heavens, was she going to make that brother of hers suffer when she saw him—she was going to keep a very long distance between her and one Leon Beaumont Esquire!

Which notion was put under a very heavy strain the next morning when, Leon already there when she entered the kitchen, he, coffee in hand, stayed, his eyes on her.

'Did I thank you for picking up a paper for me yesterday?' he asked.

Varnie was fully aware by that time that he had a better memory than anyone she knew. 'You're welcome,' she replied, turning away and going to the fridge.

'I can get my own paper today.'

That surprised her. She took the bacon from the fridge, straightened and turned to look at him. 'You're going into town?'

'I thought I might.'

'You're not working?' Now, that *was* a surprise.

'I've taken on board what you said about Jack and dull,' he replied, and there was nothing wrong with her memory either. It was *he* who had said it. She had said he should get out more, and he had come back with, 'Jack's a dull boy?'

'Shall I take a message if any business calls come through?' she enquired evenly.

'I rather thought you might come with me,' Leon announced out of the blue, to prove this was her day for surprises. 'You could take the day off too. We could have lunch in—'

'No, thanks!' she cut in shortly—that or forget all about her nagging hours of worrying if there had, after all, been anything of a sexual nature in her kiss. That or do a total about-turn on her decision to keep a very long distance between her and Leon. 'Besides which…' She ran out of ideas.

'Besides which,' he filled in for her, 'you're still out of sorts with me because of our conversation yesterday.'

She could have asked him which conversation that would be. But she knew, and to her mind he knew more than enough about the way a woman's mind worked than was good for him.

'One egg or two?' she asked shortly.

'If I apologise nicely, can we be friends?' he asked softly.

Ye gods, his charm was swamping! 'Look here, Beaumont,' she snapped, 'I might have to be engaged to you, but I draw the line at having to be friends with you as well!'

He laughed, and she had to laugh too. There was something about the wretched man. Her heart had definitely had a giddy moment just then.

He went to the study after breakfast, and she fretted briefly that he might have changed his mind about having some time off. But, after making a few phone calls, he stopped by the kitchen on his way out. 'Anything you need bringing back?'

'We're all right for everything, I think. Thanks all the same.'

He did not ask her again to go with him, but went to get

his car from the garage. And suddenly she felt flat. She wished she had said she would go with him. There was nothing to be done that could not wait.

She had anticipated he would be back within a couple of hours, but he wasn't, and Varnie went from room to room admitting that she felt dreadfully restless. And when three hours had passed, and he still wasn't back, it was with something akin to shock that she faced the fact that she missed him.

It was true that with Leon forever in the study and sometimes in the drawing room she never saw a great deal of him anyway. But he had always been in the house, and now he wasn't. And she found there was a difference.

Don't be absurd. She attempted to scoff at any weird notion that she was missing Leon, and took herself off to the attic. She had tidied and sorted out a lot of her grandfather's impedimenta, but so far the attic had remained untouched. Perhaps if she got involved in sorting through the attic she would forget any peculiar idea that Aldwyn House wasn't the same with Leon not there.

After filling several plastic bags with bits and pieces to take to the charity shop and countless old photographs of people she had never met which she intended to take to her mother, Varnie was feeling hot and dusty. She left the attic and went to take a shower.

She had just arrived downstairs when Leon came in. It amazed her more than a little how pleased she was to see him. 'Have a nice time?' she enquired, as he came into the kitchen.

'Been busy?' he countered.

'You know how it is—a woman's work is never done,' she trotted out, and felt awkward suddenly for no reason. 'Er—have you had anything to eat?'

'I have, but if there's any apple pie left...' Just that, and she was over her feeling of awkwardness. Weird—truly weird.

He was carrying a whole clutch of newspapers. But, to warm her through and through, he placed the one she favoured on top of the breadbin and went and sat at the kitchen table.

'Thanks for the paper,' she said, and unable to find a cause for her sudden feeling of breathlessness that he was not taking himself off to the drawing room to read his papers. 'You—um—you'd like your apple pie now, right?'

He glanced up, his eyes on her eyes, straying briefly to her mouth, and then back up to her eyes again, 'Right,' he said, and began reading his paper.

When later he went to the study—Varnie supposed to check the computer for some detail of business—she prepared a cold supper of meat and cheese and a side salad and left it for him.

She had an early meal herself, then started to experience a feeling of restlessness again. But it was too late to think of taking a walk—not to say too pitch black out there. She decided she might as well go to her room. Her eye caught sight of the paper Leon had brought back for her. It was as yet unread. She picked it up and, intending to read it later, took it with her.

Varnie thought about knocking on the study door and saying goodnight. And then wondered if she was going slightly dotty. She had never sought Leon out to say goodnight before—what on earth was the matter with her?

Up in her room she realised that what was the matter with her was nothing more simple than the fact that where she and Leon had started off as antagonists—he a snarling brute and she giving no quarter—they now, unbelievably, seemed to be getting on quite well.

Well, sort of, she qualified. Mostly. He could still be a snarling brute if he felt like it, and she wasn't too short on acid either. But, all in all, she found that she rather liked the brute.

As she decided that she might as well get ready for bed,

have an early night and try and catch up on some missed sleep, Varnie found she was smiling.

She had showered and was in bed—wide awake—when she remembered her newspaper. She hopped out of bed and collected it, feeling, to her bewilderment, surprisingly content. Now, wasn't that odd? She didn't want to be here with Leon, but... She turned the page over—and abruptly all thought ceased!

There in front of her was a picture of Leon, taken at some function or other—and beside it a picture of *Aldwyn House*! She read the headline and felt a jolt of shock in the pit of her stomach. There in bold print was stated, 'Tycoon's Secret Engagement'.

Hoping against hope, she read on. Oh, heavens above, it got worse. Varnie gasped audibly as she read how one of the most eligible bachelors, Leon Beaumont, was secreted away in his Welsh haven with his fiancée, Varnie Sutton.

No! It was a dreadful shock to see her name in print, her own name linked to his, and a shock to read that, because of the death of a close member of Miss Sutton's family, they were not yet officially announcing their engagement. There was more about how they had now left their haven in Wales—but as her shock evened out all Varnie could think of just then was Leon.

Had he seen the article? Was it in his paper? Or any of the bundle of papers he had brought back? Perhaps it was only in her paper? She had no idea if Pauline and Eddie were freelance people, or what they were. In any case, weren't some news items often shared or sold to other newspapers?

With the notion in her head to go and show the article to Leon, Varnie was half out of bed when she looked down at her nightdress and thought better of it. She did not feel like disturbing him clad in her nightclothes and, while she could easily have got dressed and gone to find him, she suddenly wondered if perhaps she was making too much fuss about it.

Leon was a man of the world. A man used to dealing with the press. In all probability he had fully expected something to appear in the paper today.

Yes, but what if he hadn't? What if he hadn't seen it? What if it wasn't in his paper? He had not mentioned it—and he'd been reading one of his papers in the kitchen. He had probably read the others in the drawing room. Could he be reading them right now? This very minute!

Half fearing to hear a knock at her door at any moment—though on past experience Leon was more likely to walk straight in—Varnie knew then that if Leon did not learn what was in the newspaper tonight, tomorrow morning she was going to have to tell him.

Oh, heck. Leon had said only yesterday that she had made their 'engagement' press copy when she had told Neville King that they were definitely engaged. Oh, Lord, just what had she started?

CHAPTER SEVEN

AFTER another fitful night—Varnie was finding that a guilty conscience and sleep were poor mixers—she was awake again at around five, and in a panic. Something else suddenly occurred to her, and she flung back the bedcovers and hurriedly left her bed. It was still dark out, and would be for some hours, but she knew that there was no way now that she would go back to sleep.

She switched the light on, realising that her thoughts last night had been so taken up with Leon and how he would feel about the terrible knock-on effect of her attempt to take the hurt and torment from Neville King's eyes that she had not given thought to anything else. But she could not stop thinking of something else now. And that something else was—her parents!

Oh, how could she have forgotten? Her parents took the same paper that she had been reading last night! While her father might skim-read anything headed 'Tycoon's Secret Engagement', and might miss seeing her name, her mother would not. Particularly she would not when the picture of said tycoon's 'Welsh haven' looked remarkably like a picture of Aldwyn House.

She would have to go home. Varnie knew it. She had no option. Her parents had blissfully supposed that their daughter was holidaying in Switzerland; it would be a dreadful shock to them to learn that she had instead been snuggled up in Wales with—and engaged to—some other man! A man they had heard plenty about from their son, Johnny, but whom they had never met.

Oh, grief! Varnie went and took up the paper and read the article through again. Oh, heavens, she would have to

117

go and explain. Her mother especially would be most upset when she read that her daughter and fiancé were not officially announcing their engagement yet because of the 'demise of a close member of Miss Sutton's family'. Her mother would know it must be Grandfather Sutton, and would not like at all that she had used her Grandfather Sutton's passing away in this way.

Varnie was under the shower when she began to panic anew. Surely as soon as her mother had read the paper yesterday she would have phoned her? Either at the house or, if believing the report that they had already left Aldwyn House, would have tried her mobile phone number?

By the time Varnie was dressed, in trousers, shirt and a sweater, she had calmed down sufficiently to recall that her parents might have followed through their intention now that they were retired to catch up on a lot of the pleasures they had missed when working such long hours. Namely, catching a few of the London shows. It was possible that they had spent all day yesterday in London and had not had the chance to read a newspaper. Perhaps they had caught a matinee and had dawdled back, perhaps stopping for dinner on the way. There would be nothing for them to hurry back for.

Varnie brushed her hair, applied the small amount of make-up she wore and, the time not yet six, left her room. She would collect her jacket downstairs, on her way out, but for now a more pressing obstacle loomed large. She just couldn't tiptoe out without telling Leon where she was going.

Outside her room, she hesitated. It would be much easier to write Leon a note. If she just left without seeing him then, since as far as she could remember she had never mentioned her parents, she could avoid answering awkward questions. She clearly recalled telling him that she had nowhere to live. With his phenomenal memory she doubted he would have forgotten that. She did not relish a question and answer session. But…

Impatient with herself suddenly—impatient at any idea that she might be afraid to tell him her plans to his face—Varnie went along the landing and knocked on Leon's door.

She'd anticipated he would be asleep. But when she opened his door to her surprise she saw his light was on, and that he was sitting up in bed reading. She looked across at him, her glance going from his 'To what do I owe this honour?' expression to his broad and naked manly chest. She blushed scarlet and knew not if it was from the memory of the last time she had seen his naked chest—when she had been stark naked herself—or from the fact that seeing that dark hair on his chest and his dark nipples affected her somewhat oddly.

He, however, seemed not the slightest put out. 'Why the blush?' he drawled, observing idly, 'You're dressed, so clearly I'm not in imminent threat of being seduced.'

'I knew I should have left you a note,' she said shortly, glad to feel rattled. She felt better able to handle this rattled.

'You're going somewhere?' he questioned sharply, his idle tone not staying around very long. He picked up his watch and noted the hour. 'Somewhere urgently, by the look of it,' he commented.

'I have to go to Cheltenham,' she said, in a rush.

He studied her silently for a few moments before, totally unfazed to be sitting there in his skin, he invited, 'You'd better come in and tell me about it,' and reached for his robe at the bottom of the bed. Varnie turned her head away, until he opened with another of his sharp questions. 'Are you intending to come back?' he asked bluntly.

She looked at him. He was on his feet, robe-clad, standing by his bed. 'Wild horses wouldn't keep me away,' she retorted pithily, while at the same time noticing that he had exceptionally nice legs, and wondering if her present anxieties were making her light-headed that she should think such a thing.

'Today?' Leon wanted to know. 'You'll be back today?'

Varnie nodded. She had every intention of coming back today. Indeed, she felt compelled to come back—and she hadn't even left yet!

He noted her nod and, his tone less sharp, suggested, 'Come and sit over here and tell me about it.'

Varnie felt awkward, standing there over by the door. She went forward. Bearing in mind she did not yet know what sort of lies she might have to make up—Johnny still had to be protected—Varnie reckoned that those lies could be more easily uttered were she not standing facing him.

She sat down on the side of the bed, and so did he. She felt that perhaps she was sitting a little too close, but thought to move away would draw attention to it if he had not noticed. 'So why the sudden decision? Did you know yesterday that you'd be off before daybreak but forget to tell me?' He didn't seem very pleased about that.

And *that* annoyed *her*. 'If you hadn't seen fit to give that reporter my name, and other details, I wouldn't have to go at all!' she erupted.

'My, you are uptight!'

'Well,' she huffed lamely. 'Anyhow, it wasn't until this morning, an hour ago, that the domino effect of the announcement—or non-announcement—of our "engagement" suddenly struck me.'

'You don't need much sleep either?' Leon asked conversationally, when to her mind there were more important matters here than the fact that she was awake at five in the morning.

She took a deep breath. 'There was a knock-on effect in as much as your top floor offices heard about it when I told Neville King that you and I were engaged.'

'Somebody you know in Cheltenham is likely to read yesterday's paper?'

'So you *did* read it?' she accused, but was wasting her time if she thought he would feel guilty for not telling her it had been there in the broadsheets.

'Nice picture of the house' was his only comment. Though it was sharply that he added, 'I thought you'd finished with the married Martin?'

'You thought right!' she snapped.

'So who—?'

She wanted this over and done with. 'My parents!' she cut in shortly.

'Your parents! I thought you had no one. You said—'

'Oh, shut up!' It niggled her to be caught out. 'My parents live near Cheltenham.'

'If they've disowned you, what does it matter whether you're engaged or?'

'They haven't disowned me!' she exclaimed, affronted.

'You said, and I quote, "I've nowhere to live". You're saying now that I took you in under false pretences? That you had a home all along?'

'False pretences!' Okay, so maybe she had stretched the truth a mile, more than a mile, but he'd been royally looked after. 'I've cooked for you,' she defended. 'Waited on you. Cleaned—'

'Cut to the chase,' he butted in. 'Suddenly you've parents. Why couldn't you go there—to the outskirts of Cheltenham?'

She looked away from him. To lie—or tell the truth? Johnny. Johnny—yet again. 'I told you—about Martin,' she opted for truth—so far.

'What does he have to do with it?'

'I told you I was going on holiday with him!'

'How recently?'

Shrewd as well as sharp. 'As recently as the day I arrived here,' she admitted—and at once saw a hole she was going to fall through if she couldn't think quickly. Think—think fast, before Leon trips you up. 'I was on my way back to

Cheltenham, to my parents,' she rushed on, her eyes unseeing on her knees as she sought powers of invention, 'from the airport. I—'

'I thought John Metcalfe contacted you?' Leon questioned tautly, all too clearly nobody's fool.

'He did!' she lied. 'I didn't want to go home—my mother—my parents knew I was going on holiday with Martin. I was upset, naturally, about Martin, and didn't want my parents upset too, which they would have been if they thought I was upset. So I'd stopped at a service station—when John Metcalfe, an old friend, rang my mobile and said he knew that my job in the hotel had finished and that, if I wasn't working, he needed someone to live in at Aldwyn House. I jumped at the chance.'

Leon looked at her shrewdly. 'To save your parents from worrying, from being upset that you were upset?'

Was he sounding sceptical? She couldn't decide. 'They weren't expecting me home for two weeks. I thought—hoped—that by then I would have got myself more together and would be able to pretend it didn't hurt any more.'

'It hurts—about the married Martin?'

She didn't know what that had got to do with anything, but was glad to be able to tell the truth. 'Not as much as it should had I truly been as in love with him as I thought I was. I think it was the humiliation of it more than anything. The fact that I was so taken in, so gullible.'

'Ah, Varnie,' Leon murmured, and his tone had changed, softened. He placed an arm about her shoulders and gave her squeeze of sympathy, and then removed his arm. Most oddly, she would not have minded had he left it there. 'Do you have to go to see your parents? Can you not phone them?'

She shook her head. 'My grandfather died recently. And, while I think it would have amused him, my mother will take a very dim view of my using his memory in connection with us—me—not announcing our—um—make-believe—

engagement.' Varnie's heart gave the most ridiculous flutter as it came to her that Leon was sounding very much as if he did not want her to go. She gave herself a mental shake. Ridiculous was exactly the word for it. His only concern was that he might have to make his own dinner if she wasn't back in time. 'Anyhow,' she resumed hurriedly, 'this can't be done with a simple phone call. My parents are going to worry until they see me.' She got to her feet, knowing that the sooner she started out the better.

'Drive carefully.' Leon was on his feet too, and Varnie felt quite a pang at leaving him—although she naturally pooh-poohed any such idea.

'If my parents ring here, you'll…?' Unwary, she fell into a deep hole of her own making.

'Your parents have this phone number?' Leon asked, looking at her quizzically. As Varnie knew, he had at once spotted her blunder.

'Of course not!' she found, out of a panicking nowhere. 'Forgive me. I'm going light-headed in my anxiety.'

'Calm down,' he instructed gently. 'Your parents will understand when you explain everything. I presume you intend to tell them everything?'

Varnie nodded. 'I don't want to lie to them,' she replied, but was more anxious to be away than ever now that it had dawned on her that if her parents *had* spotted that item in the paper they might ring Aldwyn House before she reached them. 'But they won't discuss it with anyone,' she assured him. She moved to the bedroom door and found Leon there beside her. She halted at the door to mention, 'There's food in the freezer….'

Leon caught a hold of one of her arms, stopping her mid-flow. She looked up into his grey eyes—when had she ever thought them cold and unfeeling? There was a warm look in them now as he interrupted, 'I won't starve,' and, letting go her arm, he smiled. It was a wonderful smile, and her heart seemed to bounce around in her chest—and that was before he added, 'Going to give me a kiss goodbye?'

Her mouth fell a little open in her surprise. Then she was unsure if he were joking. 'You know I'm not a girl like that' was the best she could do by way of repartee. But as she instantly recalled the lie of that—how she had kissed him unasked—she all at once became aware of a sudden kind of stillness about him. She was aware that he was looking at her as though something exceptionally startling had just struck him. 'Wh…?' was as far as she got.

'You're not, are you?' he said quietly. And, smart on the heels of that, 'Oh, my stars! You've never had a lover—not in the bed sense!' His voice was studded with remorse.

And Varnie knew then that he was remembering the familiar way his hands had roved her body that time, the familiar way his hands had been under her tee shirt and inside her trousers. And she espied in him, too, a fine sensitivity he liked to keep well hidden.

'Go spreading that around and you'll ruin my reputation,' she offered cheekily, her own sensitivity wanting to make light of what seemed to have shaken him.

'Hell's teeth!' he groaned. 'I must have scared the living daylights out of you! I—'

'Don't…' she hushed, and impulsively she reached up and kissed him. He stiffened, his hands coming to her arms as though to hold her off, and she was the one appalled at what she had done. 'I'm sorry, I'm sorry,' she quickly apologised. 'I didn't mean to do that. I—er—don't know what came over me.' And embarrassed that for all he had suggested she give him a kiss goodbye he must now think that she couldn't keep her hands off him, 'I know I kissed you before,' she gabbled on, 'but that was to let you know that I trusted you. You know—after that…' Oh, dash it! Her trip to Cheltenham was totally forgotten. Never had she felt so hot and bothered.

But Leon's smile suddenly came out, that wonderful

smile again, as if it pleased him that after he had been the
way he had been she trusted him. 'And now—this morning's kiss?' he asked softly.

Her spine was starting to feel as though it would melt. 'I
think—th-thought you were hurting…'

'You wanted to make me feel better?'

'Well, I—er—um…'

'What a darling you are,' he breathed, and gently then,
unhurriedly then, he took her into his arms.

Feeling slightly mesmerised, Varnie went forward. Leon
kissed her, and never before had she known such a warm,
giving, yet tender kiss. A kiss that lingered. A kiss that was
unhurried and unseeking. A kiss that was most beautiful.
Nor did those wondrous moments end with his kiss.
Because, as though Leon enjoyed having her in his arms,
he held her against him for long, long quiet seconds, before,
his hands coming to her arms, he took a step back and,
looking down into her bemused sea-green eyes, 'You'd—
better get going,' he instructed.

Where was she supposed to be going to? 'Right,' she said.

He hesitated. 'Would you like me to come with you?
Perhaps I should explain to your parents…'

Her parents! Varnie remembered everything then, and
came down to earth with a bump. 'Grief, no!' She quickly
refused the offer that would soon see her brother losing his
job. She began to back away. 'As you've said, I'd better get
going.' She went. Quickly.

She was almost in Cheltenham before she was able to
forget Leon for more than two seconds and concentrate on
what she must tell her parents. His kiss, that beautiful kiss…

She was pulling up at traffic lights when her mobile rang.
It was her mother.

'Varnie?'

'Hello, Mum. I—'

'What on *earth* is going on?'

'I'm on my way to see you.' And, panic setting in, 'You

haven't tried to get me at Aldwyn House?' she asked urgently.

'There didn't seem much point. According to yesterday's paper, you're no longer there.'

'Don't ring there. Please don't ring there,' Varnie begged. 'I'll explain when I see you. I'm less than half an hour away.'

'Yes, but—'

'The lights are changing. I'll have to go.'

It was a relief to Varnie to know that her mother had not spoken with Leon. While Varnie had learned more about the man, and in so doing hated being dishonest with him in any way, she was still concerned that she should not put her brother's job in jeopardy.

Her mother came out onto the drive the moment she heard her car arrive. Hannah Metcalfe, at fifty-five, had the same bright sea-green eyes as her daughter, was beautiful, but, unusually, was frowning as she kissed and hugged Varnie.

'Let's go inside, then you can explain all this nonsense. We went to see Aunt Crissie yesterday, and didn't get chance to read the paper until this morning. Your father spotted it—he's making a pot of tea.'

Aunt Crissie was Robert Metcalfe's sister, who lived in York. They had been promising to pay her a visit for ages, Varnie recalled. So yesterday, providentially, had been the day to keep that promise.

'I could hardly believe it!' her mother was going on. 'And where's Martin in all of this?'

'Hello, gorgeous!' Varnie's father—stepfather, that was—came out from the kitchen.

'Hello, Dad.' Varnie smiled, and knew herself much loved by both of them when the man she had only ever known as her father came over and gave her a hug and a kiss.

'I'll pour some tea, then you can tell us what you've been up to,' he said. 'Have you had breakfast?'

She hadn't, but until she had told them what she'd been up to she did not think she would be able to eat a thing. So first they went to the kitchen—only her mother couldn't wait until the tea had been poured to start asking questions. And in the kitchen Varnie told them about how she had never made it further that the airport and that Martin Walker was a married man.

'*Married!*' her mother exclaimed, horrified. 'Martin is *married*? Good heavens!' She couldn't believe it. 'Are you sure?'

'I'm sure,' Varnie replied, and relayed every word of her conversation with both Martin Walker and his secretary.

'Oh, you poor love. Are you very upset?'

'My pride was hurt, but…'

'Oh, love. Why didn't you come home?' her mother wanted to know.

'I—didn't want you to be upset.'

'As if we matter!' Robert Metcalfe scoffed, sorely wanting to use a father's privilege and flatten anyone who could treat his daughter so.

'I *was* on my way here, actually, when I thought perhaps it would be better if I went to Grandfather's house and kind of sorted myself out a bit before I came home.'

'You should have come home,' her mother said, all concern. 'If you're unhappy, your place is here with us.'

'I know, but…'

'Where does Leon Beaumont come in to it?' Robert Metcalfe wanted to know. 'There's obviously some sort of connection here with your brother.'

'Oh, there is,' Varnie replied, incapable of lying to them, but not wanting to tell tales on her brother either.

'So?' They were both obviously waiting.

'Um, Leon—Leon Beaumont—asked Johnny to find him a quiet place where he could holiday,' Varnie began carefully. 'Johnny…'

Light dawned for Johnny's father. 'Johnny contacted you

and asked if you'd consent to his boss renting Aldwyn House!' he guessed. Well, not exactly. 'He's got some nerve, that son of mine,' his father said, a hint proudly. 'You might have told us what you and your brother had arranged between you,' he commented mildly, but smiled to take any slight bruising out of his small rebuke. He went on in some relief, 'Thank goodness that young man has at last found something he's happy with and likely to stick with.'

'But—if you'd rented the house to Leon Beaumont, what were you thinking of, going there?' Her mother put the conversation back on track again. 'I know you were upset, darling, but…'

'I didn't know he'd be there.'

'Oh, I see. His tenancy wasn't due to start until later. But—you must have stayed on—' Hannah Metcalfe broke off, more interested just then in learning about her daughter's emotional state. 'How did you and he come to be unofficially engaged?'

'We're not engaged. We're not anything,' Varnie replied, trying hard to keep her mind on the conversation, which was difficult when that 'not anything' had brought a bombardment of visions of his beautiful kiss that morning. She went on to tell them, honestly and openly, about Antonia King's visit, and about the tormented Neville King's subsequent visit—and what she had done.

'*You* told him, this Neville King, that you were engaged?' her mother questioned, startled.

'Hmm, yes,' Varnie had to admit.

'Good heavens! It's a wonder Leon Beaumont didn't leave on the spot!' Hannah Metcalfe was appalled. 'And how could you refer to your grandfather as the…' That rebuke was lost when another appalling thought suddenly struck her. 'For goodness' sake, Varnie, you could have put your brother's job in danger. Oh, what were you thinking of? After all the trouble we've had with him… Now that he's at last settled, now that we no longer have to worry about him… Didn't it occur to you that Leon Beaumont could have sacked him in his absence over this—sacked him on the instant for being put in such a position?' Now did not seem a good moment to confess that Leon did not actually know that his assistant was her brother. 'And you know how much Johnny wanted that job! How he'd do anything to keep it! He's—'

'Don't go on, love,' Robert Metcalfe interrupted. 'Leon Beaumont's a grown man. He's more than capable of denying what Varnie said if it suits him. Isn't that so, Varnie?'

'It—er—suits him at the moment to be engaged,' Varnie replied. 'It was Leon who confirmed the story to the press.'

'And you're all right with that?'

Varnie nodded. 'It won't be for very long.'

'You've left Aldwyn House?'

'We're still there. Leon said we were moving on because he didn't want any more newshounds knocking on the door. I'll be going back…'

'You're going back?'

'Johnny tried to arrange for Mrs Lloyd to come and look after things, but she's retired, so I agreed to stay on and take care of the housekeeping side of everything until Leon's holiday is over,' Varnie explained.

'You're going back today?' Her mother did not look too happy about that, but otherwise accepted her explanation well enough.

'Well, not until I've sampled some of your first class cooking.'

It mystified Varnie that when she loved her home and her family, she should that day feel fidgety and want to leave it—and them. Leon was quite capable of looking after himself—more than capable, in fact—so why did she feel this emptiness, this peculiar feeling of wanting to be back there at Aldwyn House?

She stayed as long as she could. Her mother did not want her to go back at all, and pressed her to stay to an early dinner. Perversely, just to prove that she was not in any hurry to return to the property, or its present occupant, Varnie accepted her mother's offer.

It was Robert Metcalfe who nudged Varnie along when he voiced his concern about her driving in the pitch black on those dark and twisty mountain roads and suggested, 'Perhaps you'd better stay at least until morning.'

'I'll go now,' Varnie said with a smile, and was hugged and kissed by her parents, then set off for Aldwyn House, relieved that though she might have fibbed by omission here and there, she had not had to tell an outright lie to them.

It had been a sticky moment, she admitted, when it had suddenly dawned on her that, now knowing she was at Aldwyn House, either one of her parents might take it into their heads to give her a ring. And, while it was true that neither parent had met Leon, Varnie knew she would be a nervous wreck if she had to dash to be first to pick up the phone every time it rang. For what was to prevent either parent, should Leon get to answer the phone first, from introducing themselves as the parents of his assistant and also his present housekeeper?

After mulling it over for a while, Varnie had explained truthfully that Leon seemed to spend most of his holiday working, which meant she had more or less given him exclusive use of the phone.

'We mustn't interrupt big business,' her mother said lightly, having seen at once what her daughter was getting at. 'If we need to get in touch we'll ring you on your mobile. You'd better keep it charged and on.'

Varnie drove out of Gloucestershire and wished it were a more pleasant night. It had started to rain some while ago, and didn't seem to know when to stop. Still, anything was better than fog, and perhaps when she hit the mountain roads the rain would have lessened.

No chance. If anything the rain seemed heavier than ever, and came whipping across open valleys in great gusting sheets. It was certainly not a night for mere mortals to be out. Although the heavy rain caused her to drive more slowly, Varnie was at least thankful that she had the car for cover.

Her thankfulness was not to last much longer. Suddenly, to her utter dismay, her steering most unexpectedly started misbehaving. A second later, and with total disbelief, she realised she had a puncture.

No! She went into denial. She couldn't have. Her car was always in tip-top condition. Her father insisted on it and, should she forget, was always there to remind her when it was time for her car to be serviced.

By good fortune—and on such a foul night and in such diabolical circumstances Varnie felt she was due some small piece of good fortune—she was near enough to a cut-in passing area to be able to slowly steer her car out of harm's way.

Now what? For countless minutes she just sat there, as if hoping the wretched puncture would mend itself. But it was after those minutes, when not one single solitary vehicle came by, that Varnie knew she was going to have to help herself. The problem was, she knew not the first thing about changing a car wheel. In particular she did not know a thing about changing a car wheel on a pitch-black mountain road with a veritable monsoon pouring down.

Perhaps she would wait until the rain had slackened off a bit. A few minutes later it showed not the smallest sign of slackening off. Perhaps she should call someone. Leon? No way. Her father? Certainly not. By now he would be snugly tucked up in bed, miles away.

Leon was much nearer. No. Was she so feeble…? Varnie got out of the car and went to the car boot. She knew there was some kind of wheel-changing kit in there—heaven alone knew what one did with it.

Fifteen minutes later, having made a valiant attempt at undoing what she thought were called wheel nuts, she was discovering that whoever had tightened them in the first place had never intended that they should be undone. She tried again, as forcefully as she possibly could, and all to no effect—because no matter how hard she tried, and no matter how often, they just did not want to be undone.

Varnie stood up. She was drenched to the skin so it hardly mattered that the rain was still tipping down, plastering her hair to her head and face; she couldn't get any wetter.

What she *was* getting was just a mite scared—and frozen. It was eerie out there, and lonely. She squelched back inside her car and was undecided even then if, should there be another idiot out on a night like this, she would try and get them to stop. She forgot all about parables and good Samaritans and could only think of the most ghastly happenings reported by the press.

She took out her mobile phone. Better the devil she knew. By then she was past caring that she was just some feeble female unable to undo common or garden wheel nuts. Not to mention the broken nail frolic it was going to be taking one wheel off, replacing it with a spare and doing the wheel nuts up tight again—to jack the whole thing up in the process was not in her remit.

Varnie felt close to tears when she discovered that with mountains all around by no chance was she going to get a signal for her phone. Angry with her phone, the mountains, the weather, her car tyre, her own ineptitude—the list was endless—Varnie started walking, trying out her phone every fifty yards. It was a long walk.

When she did at last get a signal she was closer to tears than ever. With shaking fingers she stabbed out the phone number, hoping with all she had that he had not gone to bed, and that if he had he was not the sort who slept as soon as his head hit the pillow.

He wasn't. Almost as if he was waiting for the phone to ring, it was picked up. She did not wait for him to speak.

'Leon, I've got a puncture,' she cried tremulously, 'and I can't get the wheel off no matter how hard I try.'

To her relief he did not go in for a lecture, tell her to get lost, or demand to know what the deuce she thought she was doing, ringing to tell him about it. But, just as if he had picked up just how distressed she was, 'Where are you?' he asked calmly.

As best she could, her voice fracturing every now and then, she told him where she thought she was. 'I...' It was as far as she got.

'I'm on my way,' he cut in, and delayed only long enough to instruct, 'Lock yourself in. I'll find you.'

'You're coming...?' she gulped, but he was not there.

Varnie had no idea how long it would take Leon to get to her, but she felt cheered that she hadn't even had to ask him to come. Leon had not even suggested he would ring a garage to see if anyone would come out to her. Just 'I'm on my way' and that was it.

It was a long walk back to her car, and by the time she neared it she was feeling distressed that she'd had to bother Leon. And still the rain pelted down. Her shoes were so squelchy she was tempted to take them off. Sock clad feet could hardly be more uncomfortable.

And then, in the quiet of the night, she heard the sound of a car. She was uncertain if she wanted to be seen, and as the car rounded a bend in the road, she flattened herself against the rocks. Only to be caught in the glare of the car's headlights.

Her heart started to pound when the car driver applied the brakes urgently. Only for mammoth relief to swamp her when, nothing else on the road, the driver stepped from the car.

'L-Leon!' she gasped tearfully.

'You appear a touch damp,' he remarked levelly of her drowned rat appearance. And, reaching her, he put up a hand and gently brushed some of her sodden hair back from her face. 'Let's get you home,' he suggested mildly, and opened up the passenger door of his car and ushered her in.

'Th-thank you for coming,' she said politely, her teeth chattering. When he had nothing to say, but started the car going forward, Varnie imagined he was angry with her. 'I couldn't stay in the car. I couldn't get a signal on my mobile.'

'You're safe, that's all that matters,' he said, turning the heater up full blast. Seconds later they reached her vehicle and a place where, since they appeared to be the only traffic on the road, he could turn his car around. 'Do you need anything from your car?' he asked.

'My b-bag,' she told him through still chattering teeth.

She went to leave his car to retrieve it, but, 'Sit tight,' Leon ordered. 'I'll get it.'

Varnie sat tight, only then realising just how shivery and icy cold she was. She was hardly aware of what Leon was doing until he came back and wrapped a blanket around her.

'Every car sh-should have one,' she commented, with an attempt at humour.

'An aunt's idea of what every man should want for Christmas,' he replied, and Varnie thought she must be slightly delirious, because the words 'I love you' popped into her head and very nearly out through her mouth. She decided there and then that she had better not utter another word until she had her head back together again.

In a surprisingly short space of time Leon was pulling up on the drive of Aldwyn House. He did not waste time closing the gates or putting his car away in the garage, but came round to the passenger door and helped Varnie out.

She wanted to be in control, but did not feel in control. 'I tried to change the wheel,' she said as, with the blanket still around her, Leon propelled her through the door. She knew she had already told him that, but she wanted to impress on him that she really had tried. She did not want him to think she was feeble, as she was sure that he must. She shivered involuntarily.

'Tell me about it later. Meantime, go up and have a hot shower. Use my shower,' he instructed. 'The water pressure in yours in non-existent.'

It passed her by completely that he had obviously checked out her statement that first Saturday that there was hardly any pressure in her shower. 'It's all right. I can…' She shivered again, and all too plainly Leon did not intend to waste any time in arguing.

'Shower! Now!' he commanded, and when she just looked at him and didn't move he did no more than pick her up in his arms. For several seconds she couldn't comprehend what he was about, then he strode to the stairs with her and carried her up to his room.

Varnie was staring at him blankly when he put her down in his bathroom. 'I'll give you one minute to dump your dripping clothes and get in that shower,' he enlightened her.

Shock stopped her shivering for two seconds. 'Otherwise—you'll do it for me?' she gasped.

'Count on it!' he rapped, and put himself on the other side of the door.

Varnie wasted all of five precious seconds just staring at the closed door. A moment after that, though, and she was speedily divesting herself of her clothing.

The shower was blissful. She didn't want to leave it. Hot water cascaded down over her head and over her chilled body. Slowly she began to thaw out.

'How are you doing?'

She had company!

With no idea how much of her nakedness Leon could see through the steamed-up glass, or even if he was looking her way, she called back, 'Fine,' hoping she sounded as if it was an everyday occurrence for her to stand stark naked with just a glass partition separating her from a man she hardly knew but whom she was very much afraid she was in love with.

'Feeling warmer?'

Heavens! Love him she might, but this was embarrassing. 'Yes, thank you,' she answered primly.

'You'd better come out now.'

In a minute. 'Yes, all right,' she replied, turning the water off but waiting to hear the door into the bedroom close before she moved.

She didn't hear it close. What she did hear, and see, was the shower cubicle door slide open and an arm appear, extending a large fluffy towel. She wanted to be angry, but all at once she felt very tired, drained of energy and totally used up.

She took the towel from him and managed to wrap it round her, then stepped from the shower to find Leon, armed with a selection of towels, waiting for her. 'Wrap this one around your head,' he instructed.

In a way, for all she had never anticipated being in this sort of a situation, she was glad to have Leon in charge. She raised her arms to wrap the towel around her head, though gave a wobbly cry of, 'O-ooh,' when the towel around her started to slip.

Leon saved the day by taking a hold of the loosened end and tucking it in, his fingers warm against the swell of her breast but his manner exceedingly matter of fact. He handed her another towel and led her into his bedroom, moving her to sit on his bed. And while she sat there and dried her arms and shoulders, Leon stooped down and rubbed her feet and up to her knees dry.

By the time the rest of her was patted dry, and he had towelled her hair as dry as made no difference, Varnie was beginning to feel more than a little on another solar system. 'Who would have thought you'd have such skills?' she murmured dreamily.

'You ain't seen nothing yet,' he replied, with such a won-derful grin her heart took a flyer.

'I'll—um…' She took a shaky breath. 'I'll be all right now,' she told him.

'Wrap your hair in a dry towel,' he said, and while she was doing that he collected a towelling robe he must have found in the airing cupboard, which was now hotting up on a radiator. 'Put this on,' he instructed.

By then she was getting the picture that this was Leon's show. Quiet and authoritative, he had decided what needed to be done to prevent her from getting pneumonia and she'd better comply—or things were going to get tough.

'I bet you're a stinker at board meetings,' she complained, but when he held the robe up for her to put her arms in she stood and complied without further argument. The robe was around her when he whipped the towel beneath away. 'Goodnight,' she said. 'Er—thank you for everything.'

Leon didn't answer, but walked with her to her bedroom. 'Where do you keep your nightshirts?' he asked, on going into her room with her.

She started to feel shy, and shook her head. 'I'll sleep in this,' she decided.

He did not argue, but pulled back the bedcovers. 'Get in,' he said.

She was mesmerised and quite beyond resisting. Varnie got into bed and lay down totally exhausted. Leon brought the covers up over her shoulders. 'Goodnight,' she said again.

'Have a lie-in in the morning,' he suggested. Her eyelids were already drooping when he bent down and gently kissed her. 'Goodnight,' he added softly.

Varnie's eyelids fluttered briefly open, then closed again. She did not wonder why she loved him. She just knew that love him she did.

CHAPTER EIGHT

VARNIE slept soundly, but she slowly began to surface when some inner alarm clock nudged her at six the next morning. She did not yet feel ready to start her day, and lay there recalling Leon's instructions last night to have a lie-in in the morning. Then she recalled he had kissed her, and a smile tugged at her mouth.

She opened her eyes, but before she could focus on anything she heard a voice enquire politely, 'Do you always wake up smiling?' She jerked awake. She knew she must be dreaming, but Leon's voice had sounded so real. And no wonder! He was standing, fully dressed, right there in her room! 'I thought you might like a cup of tea,' he said, and as he came to sit on the side of her bed so Varnie struggled to sit up.

'I'll get up,' she said.

'I thought you might. But you don't have to.'

Her brains felt all over the place. Her heart was fluttering away just from seeing him. She tried hard for coherent thought. 'I had a day off yesterday,' she said, as a safe non-committal anything.

'There's no reason why you can't have today off as well,' Leon replied.

'You spoil me.' She tried for mockery.

He laughed, and floored her when he said, 'While I'm appreciative of your—luscious—um—charms, I wouldn't advise sitting up any straighter.'

Her eyes followed his—and she went scarlet. Most of the top half of her breasts were out from the covers. Another inch and her pink tipped 'charms' would be fully exposed.

Hastily she pulled the covers up. 'Where did that robe go?' she wailed.

'It wasn't me—honest,' he teased, and suggested, 'You must have felt hot in your sleep and taken it off in the night.'

'Oh,' she mumbled, but had no memory of doing so. 'Er—thank you for turning out on such a foul night and coming to look for me,' she said.

'I'd nothing else planned,' he answered easily.

'And thank you for helping me afterwards.'

'It seemed important to get you out of those sodden clothes. You were shaking with cold by the time we got here. No after-effects?' he asked. 'You're feeling all right this morning?'

'Given that I'm unused to sitting up in bed chatting away with a male of the species at six in the morning,' she began, then remembered, and smiled as she recalled, 'Though I did it to you yesterday, didn't I?'

'And without thought to bring me a cup of tea,' he complained nicely, and with a wry look, 'Nor is it the first time you've done it.' His eyes were on her face, and she blushed on recalling how she had barged into his room stark naked. Her blush must have been what he had been looking for, because he gave her a wicked kind of a grin and stood up. 'Drink your tea,' he instructed, and strolled out from her room.

Varnie watched him go, and it seemed impossible to her just then that she had ever hated him for his brutishness. Or indeed that he had ever been brutish. He was just—totally charming. Was it any wonder she was head over heels in love with him?

She sipped her tea, recalling how Johnny had said that all the women fell for Leon. But she did not want to be one of a long line of women in love with him. Though it appeared that in these matters there was very little she could do about it—other, of course, than make jolly sure Leon never saw or suspected how she felt about him.

She did not want to love him; she knew that. Soon they would go their separate ways. He would go back to London, and she would go back home to her parents. But love him she did, and had for days and days now—even though she had tried to believe she felt every other emotion for him but love. How could she be falling for him? Only two weeks ago she had thought she loved Martin.

Perhaps that was why she had tried to deny the emotion that had been waking in her for Leon. She had been ready to go away with Martin, for goodness' sake. Would have gone, had it not been for that fateful telephone call to his office.

And yet she did not love Martin. And never had. She knew that now. Knew it as she should have known it when she had not been as devastated as she would have expected to be that the man could be such a deceiver. What she did know now was that the way she had felt about Martin was totally nothing like the way she felt for Leon.

She might have *imagined* that she loved Martin, but there was nothing imagined about this powerful emotion that consumed her with regard to Leon. Not only did she love Leon, she was heart and soul in love with him. And what was she going to do about that?

There was, she knew, absolutely nothing that she could do about it. Nor was she going to sit here all day fretting about it. Varnie left her bed, made use of her temperamental shower, and got herself ready to go downstairs to see the man who yesterday she had tried to pretend meant nothing to her but who today she had to face meant everything to her.

The smell of bacon being grilled greeted her as she went down the stairs. 'You shouldn't be doing that!' she protested. 'That's my job.'

'You're having the day off,' Leon reminded her.

'You were serious?'

'Would I joke about such matters?'

She loved him in this teasing mood. 'Your holiday's done you good,' she commented—that or obey the sudden impulse to throw her arms around him and hold him close for a few moments.

'You're hinting I was like the proverbial bear with a sore head when we were first introduced?'

She grinned her answer. 'Not that from what I've seen you've had much of a break,' she said, serious as she recalled the hours he'd spent in the study. Then all at once she had the most appalling thought. 'You want me to leave?' she asked abruptly.

Leon looked at her sharply. 'What brought that on?' he demanded.

'I thought...' Her voice tailed off—she was learning that love made you sensitive, vulnerable. 'I just thought, with you cooking and everything, that you might not need me around any more,' she mumbled.

'Oh, I need you around, Varnie Sutton,' Leon replied, his expression bland. 'One egg or two?' he asked, and her momentarily dull and empty world righted itself and she burst out laughing. Hadn't she used the same 'one egg or two' question once instead of answering? Looking at him, Varnie saw his eyes were on her laughing mouth and she knew then that she was going to have to be careful that Leon did not guess how things were with her—how easily, without even trying, he could make her world bright.

'I—um—don't usually have a full breakfast,' she mumbled, in case he had not noticed.

'Today is different,' he decreed, and asked, 'What shall we do with it?'

She just loved that 'we', even if he did mean nothing by it. She glanced out of the window. It was still pouring with rain. 'How can it still be raining?' she asked. And, to answer his question, 'At a guess, I'd say gardening's out.'

Over breakfast they got down to practicalities. 'We'd better see about getting your car back,' Leon stated.

'I honestly did try to change that wheel, but the nut things just wouldn't budge.'

'You can't be good at everything,' Leon commented pleasantly.

And Varnie glowed—he must mean that she was not too bad a housekeeper. 'My clothes!' she suddenly remembered. 'I left them on your bathroom floor.'

'I dropped them in the washing machine,' Leon answered matter-of-factly. 'They were a touch wet.'

'Saturated, I'd have said,' Varnie remembered. 'You got rained on too,' she recalled apologetically. And, because she only ever wanted him to think of her as beautiful, as he had once remarked, 'Whatever must I have looked like?'

Leon leaned back and solemnly studied her for endless seconds, before he as solemnly declared, 'Not unlike one of my drowned ferrets, actually.'

She laughed. She had to. Oh, stop it, Varnie. He'll guess. But, oh, she did so love him. 'I asked for that,' she admitted, and seemed totally unable to do anything to prevent her lips from curving upwards.

Leon seemed to enjoy seeing her smile, but after a moment abruptly transferred his gaze to the grey and miserable day outside. He turned back to enquire, 'How did things go with your parents yesterday?'

This time Varnie felt she could smile freely without it being personally about him. 'They were most understanding,' she replied.

'Your mother was all right about your grandfather?'

Her mother's censure about that had been rather lost under her concern that Varnie could have put Johnny's job in danger. 'I was about to have my wrist slapped, but then something else came up,' Varnie answered, glad to be able to be truthful. But, fearing Leon might enquire further, she stood up and began taking their used breakfast plates to the sink unit, commenting as she went, 'I'd better try and find a garage prepared to go out to my car.'

'I'll go out and change your wheel,' Leon decided, joining her at the sink.

Varnie turned to glance at him. 'No, you won't,' she contradicted. 'It's still tipping it down and you'll get soaked and all messed up—and I'm feeling badly enough that through me you got a drenching last night without you getting another one today. I'll ring a garage—they'll need to take that tyre in and fit a replacement anyway.'

Leon heard her out, and then politely enquired, 'Were you the manager of that hotel?'

She blinked, not with him for a moment. Then she was smiling again—this love business was making an utter nonsense of her head. 'You think I'm a bossy boots?'

'How could I?' he asked dryly. But conceded, 'You're a spoilsport, Miss Sutton. I was looking forward to getting my hands dirty.' She turned away—she was smiling again. But she was not smiling a second or two later when, and it had absolutely nothing to do with what they had been talking about, Leon levelly let a name fall. 'John Metcalfe?'

She thought her heart would stop. 'What about him?' she asked, her knees starting to liquefy as she turned back to face him.

Leon had a look about him that suggested he was not of a mind to let up. 'You tell me?' he invited. 'You told me you had slept with him.'

Attack had to be her defence. 'That's none of your business!' she charged—and a fat lot of good it did her.

'Is he impotent?'

'How would I know?' she exclaimed, exasperated, realising only then that Leon's question no doubt came from his knowledge that she had never had a bed lover.

'How indeed?' he replied, but was grinning suddenly when he followed up with, 'You may have shared a bed with him one time, Varnie Sutton, but that's all you did.'

'Smug devil!' she becalled him, realising her quick and fast exclamation of 'How would I know?' was all the proof

Leon needed that 'slept' had been the operative word between her and his assistant.

Leon was unoffended, and was still looking pleased with himself when he commented, 'I'll get on the phone and find a garage.'

Varnie's equilibrium was restored an hour or so later. While she did a few necessary chores, and attended to the clothes she had been wearing yesterday—her shoes were never going to be the same again—Leon drove to deliver her car key to a garage some miles distant. Because the garage owner was on his own that morning he said he would go out to her car that afternoon, but that it would be of help if they could drop the key in to him. All being well her car, complete with new tyre, should be delivered to them later that day.

Leon was not yet back when the telephone rang. Varnie doubted that the call would be for her. Her parents would ring her mobile phone if they needed to contact her. So unless Russell Adams was back visiting his parents... She picked up the phone, and said, 'Hello,'—and was astonished to hear her brother's voice!

'Where are you?' she asked, thinking that he must have come home early.

'I'm in Australia.' he replied. 'What are you doing there?' he countered. 'I was hoping Leon—' he broke off. 'Oh,' he said, then, going typical Johnny whenever he was caught out, went into full confession. 'You're going to hate me, but I—ahem—rented out your property while you were away. I know, I know, no need to say it. I know I've one hell of a cheek, but—' He broke off. 'What are you doing there? You're supposed to be in Switzerland! What happened—did the snow melt?'

'I—er...' If Johnny was ringing from Australia, now did not seem the time to tell him about 'the married Martin', as Leon called him. It then suddenly struck her that if her brother had rung Aldwyn House not expecting her to be there, in that case he must have rung expecting to speak with Leon.

'Oh, you came home early,' Johnny erroneously realised. 'Well, thank goodness not too early. The thing is,' he went on, in the bubbly, effervescent way he had when things were going well for him, 'when Leon Beaumont wanted a bolt-hole, I said I knew the very place. I gave him my key to Grandfather's place, but didn't expect him to stay very long.' He paused, then enquired, 'He's not there, by any chance—?' He broke off again, and then, his voice gathering speed, 'No, of course he isn't. You both wouldn't be there. The thing is, I'm just bursting with news, but can't tell any-one until Tina has told her parents...'

Tina? Her parents? 'Slow down, Johnny,' Varnie in-structed.

'I'm gabbling, right?'

'You're gabbling.'

'Is it any wonder? I'm in love!' he sang happily.

'You're—in love?' She was doubting her hearing.

'I know it's early days yet. And I know I've only known her for a couple of weeks, but she's wonderful, Varnie. And last night we talked for hours and hours, and she agreed to marry me. Isn't that great?' He was ecstatic. 'Anyhow, Tina's parents are away until next Monday, and we agreed we'd tell both sets of parents more or less at the same time. So I can't ring Mum and Dad until Monday. You won't say anything to them, will you?'

'Er—no,' Varnie agreed, still feeling more than a degree stunned.

'Anyhow, I've been wanting to shout it from the rooftops, but knew I couldn't tell anyone. And then,' he went bub-bling on enthusiastically, 'I thought that since I don't intend to come back, perhaps I should tell Leon as early as possible so as to give him a chance to find my replacement. So...'

'Slow down, Johnny, slow down,' Varnie repeated, her

head starting to spin. 'You're saying you're not coming back to England? That you're—?'

'That's right. It's wonderful here,' he enthused. 'Tina reckons I'll soon get a job, and—?'

'You're giving up your job here!' Varnie exclaimed.

'Well, I can't do it from here—and Tina is settled in her career,' he replied. 'That's why I wanted to speak to Leon. Well, mainly to tell someone I'm getting married—someone who isn't family—but also to verbally hand in my resignation.'

'Johnny!' she exclaimed, hardly believing that after all he had said about his job with Leon—how desperate he had been to get it, how desperate he was to keep it, how it was the be all and end all of everything he had ever wanted— just like that he was ready to give it up.

'What?' he wanted to know.

'You don't think you're being a little—er—rash?'

'Oh, Varnie, please be pleased for me.'

She instantly felt guilty for putting the smallest damper on how he was feeling. 'I'm sorry, love. Of course I'm pleased for you. But...'

'I know. It's all so sudden. But love is like that. It hits you like a ton of bricks and you just know—you don't have to think about it. It's just there, swamping you.' She knew all about that. 'And driving you nuts...' He halted, and Varnie could hear his beaming smile when he sunnily suggested, 'I'm going on again, right?'

'You're entitled,' she allowed, happy for this brother who had never sounded so happy.

'You'll come to our wedding, of course. You and Mum and Dad?'

He was getting married in Australia! 'Don't you dare get married without us,' she warned.

'I won't,' he promised, and went on rapturously about his lovely Tina, sounding every bit as though he could not believe his good fortune that Tina should love him in return.

'Mind you, she'll probably want to scalp me when I tell her that I've told a member of my family about us before her folks come home. But she'll understand when I explain that I rang hoping to speak to my ex-employer...'

'Er—what are you going to do about L-Leon Beaumont?' Varnie asked.

'Nothing now. He's so busy I could ring a dozen places before I catch up with him. I'll write to him. I'll write out my resignation and post it today,' Johnny decided, but it was obvious that Tina was more in his thoughts than anyone else. And, after saying how he could not wait to be married to her, he eventually rang off.

And Varnie sat there stunned. She was, of course, happy for her brother that he had found the girl of his dreams, and she knew that her parents would be delighted too. Now that their business was sold they would have no problem with regard to being free to attend his wedding either.

But, with Leon never very far from Varnie's thoughts, it suddenly struck her that she could have passed on the message to Leon that his assistant would not be returning after his Australian holiday. And it was that thought that triggered off a whole series of thoughts that were to occupy her for quite some tumultuous while.

How could she, after all this while, now confess to Leon that she was John Metcalfe's sister? Leon would be furious with her—and she did not want that. He need never know, tempted a small voice she was inclined to listen to.

Suddenly then a whole hundredweight of implications crashed down on her. To tell Leon the truth—that she and Johnny were related by their parents' marriage—would mean telling Leon not just that but, if she were to make a clean breast of it, it would mean telling him the *whole* truth. That he was—her lodger!

No, she couldn't. How could she? While she rather thought Leon was less antagonistic with regard to women now than he had been, that still left the fact that he took favours from no one. He would be outraged were she to now confess that the woman who had been 'skivvying' for him, the woman he had allowed to cook and clean for him, actually owned the house he was living in. He would be infuriated that for the last two weeks—when he had been at his brutish worst—he had actually been beholden to her. He was a proud man. He...

Varnie shied away from telling him anything that might wound his pride, might make him angry with her. This last couple of days they had seemed to be getting on so well together. She did not want to change that. She did not want him going back to being the surly brute she had first known.

Then, all at once, as if someone had just thrown cold water over her, Varnie realised that she could leave. Leave without Leon being any the wiser! Suddenly it struck her that it no longer mattered that the wonderful job that Johnny had raved about might be in jeopardy—because her hare-brained brother no longer wanted it When he had at one time so craved to keep that job—he now no longer wanted it. She, Varnie agitatedly saw, therefore had no reason to stay! She could leave at any time she chose, and Johnny would be none the worse for it.

Oh, no, she mourned. How could she leave? She loved Leon. She wanted to stay, wanted to be near to him. She was aware that soon, any day now, he himself would leave. He had already been away from London for two weeks. True, he had been in constant touch with his office, but his 'holiday' must soon be over.

Why should she be the one to go? she argued with herself. Just a few more days with him, just a little more time with this new, warmer Leon she was getting to know—was that too much to ask? Who would she be hurting if she stayed? No one. Johnny no longer had to be protected, and it was a certainty that Johnny would not be trying to get in touch with Leon by phone again.

Oh, Leon, Leon, she pondered—and then saw his car turn

into the drive. She watched as he braked and parked his car on the drive. Watched as tall, dark, self-assured—and wonderful—he stepped from his car. And she knew then, as her heart seemed to skip a beat, that she loved him too much to go. To leave now would mean she would never see him again. Quite simply, while accepting the truth that when one of them eventually left she would never see him again, until that happened Varnie wanted more time with him.

She was in the kitchen when he came in. 'Coffee?' she offered.

'Love one,' he accepted, and the phone rang.

Varnie tensed, Even while she felt sure Johnny had no reason to ring again, she felt herself go tense in case it *was* her brother on the line. She relaxed and busied herself with making coffee when, Leon having taken the call on the kitchen phone, it turned out to be a business call.

After coffee he spent some time in the study, but an hour or so later he came to find her. 'Need any shopping?' he asked.

They could do with some fresh produce, but she was without her car. 'You'll get it for me?' she queried—it was still pouring with rain, and even if it slowed to a drizzle she was going to return exceedingly damp should she walk to the nearest small shop.

'I'll come with you,' he volunteered.

And she loved him. And she wanted to spend time with him. And anyway, she defended, it would do him good to get away from that computer. 'Now?' she accepted.

'Get your coat,' he replied.

Yesterday's jacket was soaked. She went upstairs and collected her ski jacket. 'Needs must when the devil drives,' she told him when she joined him.

'Very fetching,' he murmured, and appeared to like what he saw. But she was determined to keep her feet on the ground, so assured herself it was all part of his charm.

But charmed she was. Just the simple act of purchasing

groceries with Leon by her side seemed an adventure. Their hands touched as he handed her some bananas, and just that and she felt all wobbly inside.

Outwardly, however, she managed to appear calm and as if she was in no way affected by the good-looking man by her side. Because she had eaten a big breakfast she declined his offer of lunch out. 'Unless you're starving,' she added as an afterthought.

'I'm sure you've got something spectacular in mind for dinner,' he replied.

She laughed. 'I hope you won't turn your nose up at pork fillet with apricot stuffing?'

'As I said, spectacular,' he responded, and she so wanted to laugh again, and at the same time hold on to him, hold on to this moment, that it needed every scrap of will power to turn away.

She made a snack meal when they got back, which he ate with her in the kitchen. Leon chatted easily, and seemed to want to hear anything she had to say too, often asking her opinion.

Varnie felt flattered, and knew herself deeper and deeper in love with him the more she got to know him. And at times she felt so emotional about him she did not know how to bear it.

She was glad when later that afternoon a couple of cars turned into the gates—her car, and the car whose driver would take the mechanic back to the garage. She headed for the door. Leon was there first.

'I'll see to it,' he insisted. And, needing to be by herself for a while, Varnie let him. He did not come to see her when the two men had driven off, but went to the study.

She did not see him again until dinner. She had been upstairs to tidy herself, and would have dearly liked to have changed into one of the smart dresses she had with her. But she had not forgotten that only two weeks ago he had been fed up with one woman 'coming on to him', and by no

means did Varnie wish to see him raise his eyebrows in a
'What's this?' kind of expression when he saw her laying
the table in her best frock.

She was the one to metaphorically raise her eyebrows,
though, when, after she'd set Leon a place at the dining
room table, he appeared in the kitchen with his place-setting
in his hands. With the comment, 'You've heard of
Mohammed and that mountain,' he then laid a place for
himself at the kitchen table.

Her lips twitched. She had previously refused to eat in
the dining room with him. He had obviously decided that if
she would not eat in the dining room with him, he would,
in that case, eat in the kitchen with her.

'Feel free,' she invited casually. Casually? She was a
mess inside! 'My car all right?' she enquired, and it amazed
her that she could still *sound* so casual.

'They found a nail in your tyre.'

'A nail?'

'You could have picked it up anywhere. Something
smells good.'

It was a superb evening. Varnie lay in her bed that night
and dreamily relived every wonderful moment. Shopping
for bananas, lunchtime snack, apricot stuffing—even the in-
significant was stored up and hoarded. She had no idea when
Leon would leave—from what she had witnessed he could
as easily set up office at Aldwyn House and work from
there.

But that was just wishful thinking. If, like Johnny, Leon
had decided to take the whole month away from his office,
with luck—if she was very, *very* lucky—perhaps she would
get to share another two weeks with him. She went to sleep
hoping, oh, so much, that she would be that lucky.

The rain had miraculously stopped when Varnie got up
on Saturday and when daylight began to filter through the
dark sky a weak ray of sunshine was in there with it somewhere.

It was after breakfast when, as if he had been cooped up for far too long, Leon suggested, 'Let's walk.'

Varnie looked at him. 'You usually go walking with your skiv…housekeeper?' she asked, wondering what had got into her. For goodness' sake, she should be rushing for her hiking boots!

For answer Leon gave her a wry look. 'You stopped being just my housekeeper on the day you asked me to marry you,' he said 'Wouldn't you agree?'

Varnie opened her mouth to protest that she had never asked him to marry her. Then she closed it again when she supposed that to announce to virtually anyone who knew him that they were engaged amounted to much the same thing.

So she did the only thing left open to her. She grinned, waggled her eyebrows, and asked, 'You said yes, of course?'

Laughter lit his eyes. 'Dream on,' he jeered, his laughter breaking, and when she just had to laugh too, and just as if he could not resist it, Leon stooped and planted a light kiss on the corner of her mouth.

Her knees felt ready to give way, but somehow she managed not to crumble, and, as he had ordered yesterday, 'Get your coat,' she ordered.

That day was one of the best days of her life. And, if possible, she fell even deeper in love with Leon. They talked, they laughed, they walked, and were serious. Sometimes, when they were passing over rough ground, Leon would touch a hand to her elbow, guiding her. That she needed no guiding was neither here nor there; she loved the feel of his touch.

It was as she relived that day when she went to bed that night, though, that she began to grow anxious that Leon might have glimpsed how it was with her. She'd just die of mortification if he had.

When she got up the next morning it was to find her

anxieties of the previous night were still with her. She loved him, that was true. But he did not want her love. Neither was he interested in her in any way other than perhaps as a companion while he was away from his home and friends.

Come to think of it, he had once suggested that they be friends, but... Varnie started her day feeling uneasily that maybe she, purely in her love for him, had been too forward with Leon yesterday. And that, in turn, made her feel uncomfortable with him.

So much so that she kept out of his way as much as possible. When he strolled into the kitchen she found she had to be doing something somewhere else. She was dusting the drawing room when he came in with the Sunday papers he had been to collect.

'Just finished,' she announced, looking anywhere but at him. 'I'll leave you to it.'

He looked at her quizzically. 'I got a paper for you,' he said evenly.

'Oh, lovely,' she replied. 'Thank you.' And, taking it from him, she took it with her to read elsewhere.

By lunchtime she had run out of jobs. She had a sandwich herself, and prepared a snack lunch for him that she took into the drawing room on a tray. Then she took herself off to the garden and, the ground still wet, attempted to tidy up.

She glanced to the house. Leon was watching her from one of the drawing room windows. She wanted to be in the drawing room with him, and was at odds with herself, even with the love she had for him, that when yesterday she had been so comfortable just to be with him, today she should feel so awkward.

But she resumed her gardening efforts and would not go in. Leon had been off women 'in spades' when he'd arrived, and she did not want to be like any of the women who sought him out, or who had caused him to be so fed up he had sought the solitude of a place like Aldwyn House.

Varnie kept out of his way for the rest of the day. Having

put her gardening tools away, she decided to take her car for a test run—for all she was sure the replaced wheel had been accurately positioned.

She eventually returned, knowing that dinner was going to be a problem. It would be too farcical after they had eaten in the kitchen yesterday and Friday to now start laying a place in the dining room for him.

They did eat together, but she hated that she could no longer be natural with him. He would just love it, wouldn't he, if he knew how she felt about him? So, in her attempts to show him that she did not care, she found she smiled less—in fact her smile was non-existent. And soon any conversation between them petered out.

Last night he had helped with the washing up. That night, as soon as he had eaten all that he wanted, he pushed back his chair, grunted his thanks for the meal, and took himself off elsewhere.

And Varnie straight away wished that things had been different. But she washed and dried dishes and knew that they could not be different. She tidied the kitchen and then had several choices: stay where she was, go to the drawing room—where Leon was—or go to bed.

She opted to go upstairs. Sadly, she somehow had an idea that Leon would be quite relieved to have the drawing room to himself.

But it was early, and she was restless and could not settle. She decided to take a shower. Then she realised she had removed the towels from her bathroom earlier and had not replaced them.

She left her room and headed for the airing cupboard, and had a grasshopper brain moment when she spotted the freshly ironed shirts there belonging to Leon. It took but a moment to gather the warm shirts up. Closing the airing cupboard doors behind her, Varnie went along to Leon's room. By the time he came up to bed his laundry would be ready for him to put away.

She supposed her brain must still be a degree on other matters because, when she usually left his clean laundry outside his door, that evening without so much as a thought to knock she went straight in—and stopped dead.

'Leon!' she gasped, seeing the man she so loved standing there for all the world as though he had been pacing his room and had halted, equally surprised to see her. 'I'm s-sorry,' she stammered, regaining some of her composure. 'I didn't know you were in here.'

'Obviously,' he retorted shortly.

And while she wanted to hurriedly back out, because he clearly did not care for her walking in unannounced, she considered it would be totally undignified to back out and place his shirts outside his door.

'Forgive me,' she said stiffly. 'It won't happen again.'

'I wasn't referring to you coming in here,' Leon told her curtly, 'but to the fact that it's plain for anyone to see that you'd rather be anywhere that I am not,' he ended coldly. And suddenly Varnie was appalled.

'Oh, Leon,' she wailed. 'It's not you!'

'Not?' he demanded, his expression not lightening at all. 'What, then? You've been avoiding me like the plague all day. I was close to coming to find you. If I've upset you in some way, don't you think I've a right to know how?'

'Oh, Leon,' she said again, and had to smile. A fortnight ago he would not have cared one whit about upsetting her. Yet tonight he had been near to coming to find her! That did not mean he cared anything now, of course, warned a sobering voice that she knew it would be better if she listened to. 'I…' she said helplessly. Suddenly it was all mixed up in her head. 'You came here because you were fed up about women—well, that was part of your reason anyway…' She attempted to straighten it. 'And it—I—er—well, I—' She broke off and discovered then that love meant not wanting to upset that someone you loved. And even though her head scoffed that her attitude that day could not have upset Leon in any small way, she found she was confessing openly, 'I enjoyed being friends with you. But I got to wondering if—considering how you'd felt about women—if—if I'd been, well, a bit too friendly.'

Leon looked astonished. 'As in—come on to me, you mean?'

She wasn't sure what she meant any more. She felt hot and all of a jangle inside. 'Sh-shall I put your shirts over here?' she asked, heading for the chest of drawers. He did not answer, and she went and placed his clean laundry down on top of it and turned about. But suddenly she did not want to go to bed bad friends with him. A yard or two away from him she stopped, and held out her right hand. 'I'm sorry,' she apologised. 'I'd like to be friends while we're here.'

Leon shook his head. 'What a mixture you are,' he said softly, all animosity gone from him. And, coming over to her, he caught hold of her hand in his—not to shake it, but to hold as he looked down into her apologetic lovely sea-green eyes. 'I'll forgive you,' he said with a smile, and bent his head to lightly touch his lips to hers. She had tingled just from the fact he was holding her hand—and that was before he kissed her. 'You kissed me once to show you'd forgiven and trusted me,' he reminded her.

She wanted to kiss him again, but knew that she must not get carried away by her emotions of the moment. 'Yes, well…' she mumbled, and took a step away from him because that was the sensible thing to do. But who said love was sensible? Especially when she looked up into his grey eyes that seemed warm and all sensitive to her.

Hardly aware of what she was doing, she took a step to him again and stretched up and kissed him—and immediately felt embarrassed that she had. She searched desperately for some sane reason for doing what she had, when sane reason there was none.

'There,' she said, as lightly as she could, 'that makes us quits.' She went to move away, because that was the sen-

sible thing to do, and what she knew she must do. But somehow her feet seemed glued to the spot and Leon, his eyes
holding hers, seemed to have quite liked the touch of her
lips against his, because the next she knew, to her utter joy,
he was gathering her into his arms.

'I'm not so sure that it does,' he murmured, and, his head
coming closer, he again touched his lips to hers. 'What do
you think?' he asked, raising his head.

Varnie was by then feeling too bemused to think clearly
about anything. 'Do—um—friends usually kiss like this?'
she asked, knowing that it would be a bright idea to move
out of his hold, but loving the feel of his arms around her
too much to want to listen to any bright ideas.

She supposed Leon must have taken as encouragement
that she was still standing there, for he smiled a slow kind
of smile, a heart-melting kind of smile, and softly assured
her, 'Oh, yes, friends do.' And, to her delight, 'More than
friends kiss like this,' he added, and his head came down
once more, and Varnie was on the receiving end of a kiss
that was in no way platonic.

She gasped from the thrill of it, and realised when he
stood tall again that there was only one thing she could do.
She did it. She placed her hands on his waist and told him
impishly, if admittedly rather huskily, 'You do that again,
Mr Beaumont, and I won't be responsible for the consequences.'

He heard her out, and then laughed a warm, pleased, yet
seductive laugh. And when his head came near she was *not*
responsible for the consequences—she was quite unable to
think straight anyhow as he gathered her closer to him. Her
lips parted to receive his kiss, and as he accepted their de-
lights, his own lips parting to enjoy hers, Varnie put her
arms around him.

She held on to him, loving him with all of her heart.
'Sweet Varnie,' he breathed, and, feeling her full response,
deepened his kiss.

He held her yet closer to him, and she was enraptured to be held close up against his hard male body. 'Leon!' she whispered shakily, and he pulled back to search her face.

'Problem?' he asked gently.

'Only when you stop,' she answered, and did not care a bit then that she might sound forward, because Leon grinned, as though enchanted by her, and claimed her mouth once more.

Ageless minutes ticked by where she was totally enthralled by Leon, by the kisses he gave and took. She was enthralled just to be in his arms, held near to the man who held her heart. She loved the touch of him, his lips, his hands, his kisses to her throat—she simply adored him.

As she adored too the way, after some gentle while, his hands at her waist began to explore the hem of the tee shirt she had on. He wanted more—and so did she. She clutched on to him when she felt his warm touch as his hands and fingers negotiated their way beneath her tee shirt.

She kissed him, to let him know she loved the feel of his touch on her ribcage, but held on to him tightly when that same touch, those same hands caressed their way to her breasts.

'Relax, sweet love,' Leon instructed. And, teasingly, 'Or I shall have to stop.'

'Oh, Leon!' she cried, glorying in this sudden freedom, and kissed him again. And she had not the smallest objection to make when he unfastened her bra; the better to caress her. 'Oh!' she exclaimed, as sensitive fingers traced over the hardened peaks of her breasts and sensitive palms supported and moulded the swollen globes.

She placed her hands on his shoulders, dizzy with the riot of emotions he was creating in her—and a few moments later she could hardly believe that he had taken advantage of her raised arms to take her tee shirt from her.

'Oh!' she cried, in panic this time, and swiftly placed her hands over her breasts to hide them from his view.

But by then Leon had divested himself of his shirt, and her panic faded under the wonder of seeing his naked chest.

'I want—to touch you!' she gasped.

'Touch me, sweet Varnie,' he invited.

In the spell of the powerful emotions he had awakened in her, Varnie forgot all about her hands being the only cover to her breasts. And she stretched out both her hands—one to stroke and caress the silken hair on his chest, that intriguingly formed a line down to the waistband of his trousers, the other to investigate his nipples.

She stared at his chest in wonder. Then all of a sudden realised that Leon was looking his fill too, at her, when hoarsely he murmured, 'Oh, sweetest love, you are just sensational.'

Colour rioted through her face, and she realised that it was for her, and not him, that he pulled her close and hid her breasts from his view. He kissed her again, gently at first, then all at once there was a new kind of element in his kiss, a passion that was building and building. And as that passion fired him to draw her against him, so the feel of her breast against his naked skin seemed to inflame him to a yet deeper passion.

When his lips left hers it was only so he could bend and touch his lips to the throbbing pink nub of her left breast while one hand teased and tormented the other.

'Oh, Leon,' she cried. 'I've never felt like this before.'

'You want me?' he asked softly.

'Yes,' she whispered shyly, and was drowning in yet more kisses, in yet deeper emotions, as his hands came to the fastening of her trousers.

Varnie kissed and clung to him, her heart racing at this new world she found herself in. Then her bare legs came into contact with his bare legs, and it was with wonder that she realised that as well as her trousers, Leon's trousers too had vanished.

'Leon…' She said his name as something—she didn't think it was panic—started to attack her.

'Don't worry, my darling,' Leon instructed. 'I'll look after you.'

She looked into his eyes. They were warm, giving. And the thrill of being called his darling made the moments they were sharing magical beyond belief. So she smiled at him, giving him her absolute consent to take her wherever he chose.

And that place, a minute or so later, was to his bed. His mouth was over hers when he picked her up in his arms and carried her to his bed. And Varnie thought her heart would burst with her love for him when he kissed her, caressed her and rolled to her, and she felt his hard body over hers.

Her legs parted of their own volition to give him comfort, and he slid between the welcoming warmth of her thighs, his eyes holding hers as he tenderly stroked down the side of her face. And she just had to tell him, 'I want you so much. I never knew I could want…' Her voice trailed off.

'Sweet darling,' he breathed, and, considerately, 'We'll take it slowly.' And with that he kissed her, so tenderly, so lovingly, that she almost could not bear it.

She wanted so badly to tell him of her love for him. To tell him just how much she was heart and soul his. That for love of him— Abruptly, like a douche of iced water, in the midst of deepest passion—when she had thought she was ready to be his any time he chose to take her—Varnie suddenly, and not a little bewilderingly, had a moment of stark sanity.

Tell him she loved him! Had she gone mad? Had he asked for her love? Did he want her love? No! This, for him at any rate, was not love. Love, as far as Leon was concerned, had no part in what they were doing, were about to do.

'No!' she cried on a note of panic, and, hardly able to think straight, she pushed at him.

To his credit, Leon raised his body and put some daylight

between them. 'No?' he queried, to her ears sounding slightly stunned.

'I—c-can't,' she told him agitatedly. She still wasn't thinking straight, but some inner self was working her strings. Pushing away from him, she edged over to the side of the bed, her head and heart in turmoil.

She heard him take a deep and controlling breath, and his voice when it came was soothing, quiet, as he said, 'There's no need to panic. We have all night to…'

She felt herself weakening. She wanted him so badly. 'I'm—s-sorry,' she mumbled jerkily, and dared not look at him, knowing only that she was weakening fast and that should she look at him she would lose her hold on what she instinctively knew was the right thing to do. 'I—just— c-can't,' she choked, her voice cracking.

And, acting while she still could, she shot to her feet and ran from him to her own room, and slammed the door hard shut in case she should weaken and go back.

Then she began to fear that Leon might follow her and resume making love to her in her room. Her will power was used up—she knew she would not resist him.

But she need not have worried. Leon did not follow her.

CHAPTER NINE

THAT night seemed never-ending. Varnie knew that she had done the right thing, and that to flee Leon's room had been the only thing to do. But she was fast discovering that doing what her head said was the right thing did not hold any sway with her heart.

In her heart she wanted to be back with him. Wanted to be back in his room with him. Wanted to be held by him and kissed by him, and to blazes with the harsh reality that he cared nothing for her.

Her first impulse was to pack her suitcase without delay and to get out of there. But in her heart she did not want to leave.

Yet, what point was there to stay? 'I've had it with clinging women,' he had told her once. Was that what she had become—another of his clinging women?

Her pride reared up. She wanted to ignore her pride. But it badgered away at her. Was she to stay only for the same situation to arise again? She had wanted Leon to make love to her, and on his part he had desired her; she knew that he had. So if that mutual wanting was somehow triggered again—no matter how much they might determine it would not—what then? Two weeks maximum of their sharing each other then, Hey-ho, London calls, it's been nice knowing you. I don't think so.

It was many tortured hours later that Varnie gave in to what she knew, and had known, she must do. Johnny no longer figured in the equation, though she had an idea that she would have reached the same decision had he still been desperate to keep his job. Thankfully, he was not.

On Friday she had realised that she loved Leon too much

to leave. At around five that Monday morning Varnie knew that she loved him too much to stay.

She wanted to go, and go now. All at once it seemed urgent that she left without seeing Leon again. She mourned the fact that she would never see him again. But what was the point of waiting until breakfast time to tell him that she was leaving? It was highly unlikely that he would try to prevent her from going.

Varnie shrugged out of the robe she had put on when she had realised that she was as near naked as made no difference. Colour flared to her face when she recalled how, with not a stitch on apart from her lacy briefs, she had run from Leon.

Wanting to now be away with all speed, she dressed and knew that she could not leave without some note of explanation. But what excuse was there?

Feeling impatient with herself, and not a little unsure that she might not be using delaying tactics, Varnie took out her pen, found a scrap of paper and wrote simply, 'Dear Leon, I think it best that I should leave.' She signed it 'Varnie', and, knowing that she had made the right decision but fearing that her need to see his face just one more time might weaken her, without stopping to pack, she took up her bag with her car key and noiselessly left her room. She placed her note on top of the stairs, and, as silently, let herself out of the house.

Her soft-soled shoes made not the smallest sound as she walked to the end of the drive and opened the gates. Thankfully she had not garaged her car, so all she had to do was to open it with her battery-operated key, slide inside, and be away.

It was still dark when she arrived at the borders of Gloucestershire. She wanted to go back to Wales. She felt bereft, and did not feel any better to know that this was the way it was going to be.

Her parents were early risers, and were up and about

when she went in. Varnie pinned a smile on her face, but found that for the moment her parents had too much else on their minds to notice that something might be amiss with her world.

'Couldn't you sleep?' was her father's cheery comment, referring to the fact that she must have got up before the birds to have got there so early. 'We were just thinking of ringing you.'

'Did you know about this?' her mother asked before Varnie could reply.

Her mother was smiling. 'What?' Varnie asked.

'Johnny's just phoned,' Robert Metcalfe replied. 'He's getting married.'

'Oh!' Varnie exclaimed, but confessed, 'Johnny wanted to tell you first, only he rang to tell Leon—Beaumont—that he was resigning and I answered the phone.'

'He's met this most wonderful girl, apparently. He can talk of nothing and no one else but Tina. He wants to get married as soon as it can be arranged, and wants us to go out there as soon as we can!' her mother went on, but then suddenly realised, 'You've left Aldwyn House? Or are you going back?'

'Leon doesn't need me,' Varnie replied, and could have wept at the truth of that.

But matters pertaining to Johnny and his surprising news were to the forefront of her parents' minds, and while the three of them sat down to breakfast together Robert and Hannah Metcalfe laid plans for a trip to Australia.

'You'll come with us, of course.' Her mother stated it as a foregone conclusion. 'We'll have to wait until nine o'clock for the travel agents to open....'

A half-hour later everything was more or less agreed upon. Robert Metcalfe had his bi-yearly eyesight test scheduled for nine-thirty that morning, his wife would go with him, and they had decided they would call at the travel agents after his eye test, and make enquiries about travelling in about a month's time.

'You look tired,' her mother suddenly observed. 'You must have got up early to avoid the traffic. You needn't come with us unless you're desperate to. Dad can arrange everything for you. All right?'

'Yes. Fine,' Varnie answered, trying to show enthusiasm, but her heart and head were more in Wales than on the Australian trip.

The house was quiet after her parents had gone, and Varnie was glad to not have to pretend that everything was roses in her world. 'Leon doesn't need me,' she had told her mother, and that about summed everything up. While she needed him, he did not need her. And she had been right to leave. Had she stayed, had he kissed her again, she would not have had the strength to tell him no a second time. Even now she wanted again to feel his arms around her.

Varnie went up to her room and showered and changed into fresh clothes. She tried to feel glad that she was home again, home in familiar surroundings where she knew she was loved, but her heart wasn't in it.

Time seemed to drag. So much had happened and it wasn't yet ten o'clock. She decided to keep busy, and to that end went down the stairs and took a look in the fridge, thinking to have lunch ready for when her parents returned. She closed the fridge door when someone rang the front door bell.

She went along to the front door, not too curious to find out who was calling or what they wanted. But, on pulling back the front door, she nearly dropped with shock! Leon Beaumont stood there! Hot colour surged to her face.

He eyed her steadily for several long seconds, taking in the swift tide of colour that flushed her face. Varnie had still not recovered or found her voice when slowly he drawled,

'I think you and I have a little unfinished business, Varnie Sutton.'

She felt brain dead. 'If it's about my bonus, you can keep…' was the poor best she could manage by the way of sauce, and her voice tailed off at the sudden glint in his eyes.

'Perhaps "business" was the wrong choice of word,' he answered evenly. And, fixing her with a deliberate stare, as if waiting, watching, for her reaction, 'It's more personal than that.'

Instinctively she wanted to slam the door closed on him. He couldn't know she loved him, could he? He mustn't know that she loved him. 'I think we were more "personal" last night than employer and employee should be!' she retorted, and could hardly believe that she was so shaken to see him standing there on her doorstep, when she had never expected to see him again, that she was actually referring to their lovemaking of the previous evening! 'You must have left around six o'clock to have got here so quickly,' she remarked, desperate to change the subject, but still struggling to surface.

'You're blushing again,' Leon commented easily, appearing far more at home than she was feeling. 'Half past, actually,' he replied, and asked, 'What time did you leave?'

'Fiveish,' she replied.

He nodded. 'Around the time I nodded off to sleep for the first time,' he stated.

Varnie's eyes widened a touch. Was he saying that he'd had the same sleepless night that she'd had? Well, not for the same reason, obviously, huffed a down-to-earth inner voice.

'You—I—didn't think you knew where I lived.'

'I didn't,' he answered, and added with no small hint, 'It's a long story.'

Only then did Varnie become aware of her rudeness in keeping him standing there on the doorstep. She did not want to invite him in. Yes, she did, of course she did, argued the heart that loved him. She had thought never to see him again.

'You'd better come in,' she said, heart winning with a touch of manners over a head that warned no, that if she did she would have to guard that he did not guess at her feelings for him. 'I'm—um—afraid my parents aren't in,' she apologised as she led the way to the sitting room.

'No matter,' Leon answered. 'It wasn't your parents I came to see.'

'W-would you like a coffee after your drive?' she enquired politely, reaching the sitting room and belatedly doing her hostess bit as she turned to face him. He must have been driving for over three hours.

'I'd prefer to have a few honest answers,' he replied, which well and truly threw her.

'Honest answers?'

'Could you not bring yourself to be honest with me for once?' he asked, his expression serious.

His serious expression worried her somewhat. He seemed somehow like a man who had set out on some sort of course and looked unlikely to veer from it—as in he wanted some honest answers, and would not desist until he had those honest answers.

'T-take a seat,' she invited, while she quickly mulled over his request. She supposed, up to a point—that point being to see he had no clue about her true feelings for him—that she could be honest with him. Leon went over to one of the two sofas in the room, but, his manners on show too, waited until Varnie took a seat on the other one. They were both seated, Leon looking across at her, when Varnie, a shade reluctantly, admitted, 'I suppose I have been a—touch—um—less than truthful with you.'

'A touch? Only a touch?'

'I didn't think I'd lied all that much,' she retorted sniffily, not liking to be put on the defensive.

'What about lies of omission?' he asked quietly.

She had no idea just how much he knew about her lies of omission, or her lies either, for that matter. But to have found out where she lived indicated that he knew more than she had thought. But this was her home—she tried to get angry—he had no right to come here and disturb her. Varnie was realising that she would be putty in his hands if she did not find some backbone to attack.

'What about you?' she erupted. 'You were a real pain when I first met you. You didn't actually invite truthful confidences!'

He smiled. It was a small smile, and soon disappeared, but it warmed her heart to catch a glimpse of it, and that was before he agreed. 'Guilty as charged.'

'Yes, well,' she mumbled, and then got herself more of one piece. 'How much do you know?' she asked.

'You're saying you intend to lie about the rest?'

She had to laugh. 'Oh, shut up,' she protested, and loved him so desperately when he grinned, every bit as though he enjoyed her company, enjoyed her laugh. 'No, don't shut up,' she countermanded, getting herself back together again. 'Tell me how the Dickens you knew where to find me?' And, as the thought suddenly struck, 'And why you bothered to find me anyway?'

Leon looked levelly at her for some moments before, as if making up his mind to face up and be truthful himself, even if she would not, 'The one was easy, the other…' He left it there, but did go on to state, 'At the risk of making you blush again, you'll accept, I think, that we were both rather led by our emotions last night.'

If he meant physical emotions she was prepared to agree, although for her, her heart was involved too. 'Yes,' she conceded quietly.

Leon gave her a warm look for her honesty, and continued, 'I don't know what kind of a night you spent, or how much sleep you got, but it wasn't until five this morning that I had to force myself to lie down and make myself go to sleep. That,' he said, looking directly across at her, 'or give in to the compulsion I'd battled with ever since you ran from me to come to your room and try to comfort you.'

'You—wanted to—comfort me?'

His smile was gentle. 'I knew you were upset—I've learned a little of you these past couple of weeks. I knew you'd never been that far with any man before. You'd said you'd never felt the way you did before. Yes, I wanted to comfort you.'

'But you made yourself stay put?'

'I had to. It was never my intention to make love to you last night. It just sort of happened,' he confessed. 'There's a chemistry between us Varnie, that causes you as well as me, I think, to go into realms we'd not thought of going.'

Varnie stared at him and half wished she knew as much as he did. 'So you made yourself stay put in case that— ch-chemistry—um—stirred again?'

Leon nodded. 'And then we'd be back to square one.'

She smiled at his thoughtfulness. 'So you stayed where you were?'

'Lord what a night it was,' he took up. 'It was around five this morning when I knew that if I could hang on for another hour you would be getting up anyway and I made myself get on my bed. Just one more hour, then I'd go downstairs, and soon, away from our bedrooms, you would join me.'

Varnie wished she had known that Leon was spending the same fraught night that she had wearied through. Though perhaps matters had worked out for the best. Had he taken her in his arms again, in her bedroom or in the kitchen for that matter—in a hold of comfort or whatever— who knew what chemistry might not have erupted between them?

'You went to sleep around the time I left?' she offered.

'I swear I slept no longer than ten minutes before I was

awake again, and again enduring the torture of waiting for
six o'clock.'

'You left your room around six?'

'And just couldn't believe my eyes when I found your
note.' He looked at her solemnly then, and after some moments commented slowly, 'You may have thought it best to
leave, Varnie Sutton, but I didn't.'

'Oh,' she murmured, and tried her hardest not to read
anything there that simply was not there. 'Well, you can't
be thinking of staying at Aldwyn House for much longer.
And, from what I've seen you're quite able to look after
yourself. And in any case there's plenty of foodstuffs in the
freezer. All you—'

'The freezer may be full.' He cut her off—and very near
shattered her when quietly he added, 'But the house is
empty—without you.'

Her mouth felt dry, and her heart started to pound, and
Varnie was having the most dreadful time in trying to tell
herself that Leon did not mean anything at all by that last
statement. It must be all very much part of his charm. And
yet—he was looking at her very much as if he *did* mean
something, that he *did* feel that the house was empty without
her.

'Um—well, I would have left at some time...' she attempted.

'But not before I had a note of your address,' he butted
in. He wanted to know where to contact her? Oh, heavens.
'You arrive in the dead of night,' he went on, as if laying
a charge at her door, 'and depart in the dark of early morning, with not the smallest intention of letting me know
where you're going. Do I mean so little to you?' he demanded.

Oh—keep away from there! No way was she going to
tell him what a very great deal he meant to her. 'How did
you find my address?' she asked, sheer desperation to hide

what a very great deal he meant to her bringing a diverting question.

Leon stared unsmiling at her, and she thought for several panicking moments that he was going to press for an answer to his question before he answered hers. But all at once he seemed to relent, just as if supposing it was a question he could go back to when her question had been dealt with.

'I rang John Metcalfe,' he said simply.

'You ra…! *In Australia!*' she gasped. And, while her brain tried to cope with what Johnny might or might not have told Leon, 'I didn't know you had his phone number.'

'I didn't,' he agreed. 'But he was the only person I knew whom I thought would have your address—or at the very least your phone number.'

Oh, my word. Varnie took a steadying breath, trying not to read anything ridiculously hopeful into Leon seeming a touch keen to contact her. 'You didn't have his Australian number, you said?' Take it slowly, Varnie, she advised. You could fall flat on your face at any moment.

'I rang my PA.'

'At six in the morning!'

He shook his head. 'I pointed my car in this direction and rang her at seven.'

He had followed her? Without knowing where she lived—his only clue being that she lived Cheltenham way— he had followed her! 'Your PA had Johnny's number?'

'Not with her. It's company policy for senior management to leave a contact number when they go on holiday,' Leon explained. 'While Metcalfe doesn't have that status, I was hoping that Evelyn had been her usual ultra-efficient self and had included Metcalfe because, basically, he works from the top floor. She rang me as soon as she reached the office.'

'You rang him from your car?'

'I thought I'd better do it from a landline. I stopped at a hotel.' Leon paused, his eyes watchful, then he went on,

'He tells me he's getting married. In fact he's so animated about it I had a hard job prising him away from that subject to tell me what I wanted to know.' Leon's gaze was thoughtful. 'How do you feel about it?' he asked. 'Metcalfe getting married?'

'I'm very pleased for him,' Varnie answered truthfully.

'You are? You knew he was getting married?'

Varnie did not understand his severe expression, but smiled and quite without thought stated, 'That's part of the reason for my parents being out just now. They're checking on flights for our trip to Australia to see him married.'

Leon stared at her. 'Your parents know him too?' he questioned. Then bluntly, a touch aggressively, she thought, 'Don't you think it's time you told me what the hell has been going on?'

In her view she did not owe him an explanation, and had no need to tell him anything. Against that, though, she loved the wretched man. 'I—um—haven't been totally honest with you,' she confessed.

'Tell me something I don't know!' he grunted, and, plainly sifting through what he so far knew, 'How did you know Metcalfe is getting married? He hadn't met the girl before he left for Australia. Ah—he rang you on your famous mobile!'

'Famous?'

'I got to thinking it was very convenient, Metcalfe phoning you more or less at the same time that you were dumping the married Martin,' Leon replied, going on to challenge, 'Metcalfe didn't ring you when you were *en route* from the airport, did he?'

Varnie stared at Leon and felt a nervous laugh rise to her throat. 'To be honest, no.'

'Hmph!' he grunted. 'And all that guff about not wanting to come here because you didn't want your parents to witness your upset was just so much baloney?'

'No!' she denied. 'That was true. I *was* on my way home

when I thought about my parents—they'd had a bit of a stressful time recently. I decided to lick my wounds at Aldwyn House instead.'

'You'd stayed there before,' he documented, and, as intelligent as ever, 'You thought the house would be empty and knew where to find the key.' He halted, and then questioned, 'Don't you think you were taking a bit of a risk?'

Oh, heck, there was nothing for it. Retribution was here— but if she were going to go down, it would be with colours flying. 'There was no risk, so far as I was aware at the time,' she replied. 'Nor was there any need for me to look for a key. I already had a set of keys.' She wished she felt as cool as that had sounded. 'I...' She coughed. The moment was unavoidable now. 'I—um—own the place,' she brought out faintly.

Silence, deathly silence greeted her announcement. 'You *own* Aldwyn House?' Leon demanded harshly.

'My grandfather—I told you he had recently died—he left it to me.' Oh, grief, Leon's expression was grim.

'Let me get this straight,' he said toughly. 'I've been living in *your* house? The property I've been living in is *owned* by you?' And, with anger there, 'Why the blazes didn't you tell me? Why, in thunder...? Hell's bells, you've—cooked and cleaned for me! You—'

'It wasn't so bad.' She attempted to interrupt. 'H—'

'*Talk!*' He cut her off. 'Start talking—and make it the truth!' he rapped, and, his quick-thinking mind there again, 'Why, for instance, if as you say it's your house, does Metcalfe have a key he can hand out to all and sundry?' he demanded.

Any sign of her trying to appear cool promptly fell away. 'He—um—didn't know I would be paying a visit,' she mumbled.

'And?' Leon was relentless.

'And—er...'

'The key?'

'I—um—gave it to him—er—some while ago,' she owned. Oh, heavens, Leon was back to being the way he had been when she had first met him.

Her initial instinct was to revert to the snappy way she had been too. But she had got to know him a little, and, aside from being deeply in love with him, she knew he had a more sensitive side.

'And...' she began again, but did not know quite where to start.

Leon was there again, leaving the issue of her giving John Metcalfe a key in abeyance for the moment, but pressing determindly for more information just the same. 'You didn't know I was there—at Aldwyn House?' He kept up his interrogation.

'It was a bit of a shock to see you there,' she mumbled, feeling a familiar pink around her ears as she recalled trotting into his room stitchless. 'A lot of a shock, actually.'

Leon observed her high colour. But then something else struck him. 'You weren't expecting me to be there *at all*? You thought—believed—were sure—that you'd have the house all to yourself!' He stared dumbfounded at her, before accusing, 'As far as you were concerned I was an interloper!'

Varnie didn't know what to say to make it better. 'It—er—as I said, it was a shock to see you there. But I knew who you were,' she hurried on. 'I'd seen that picture of you in the paper, thumping Neville King.'

'Why didn't you tell me to clear off?' Leon wanted to know. 'You didn't know at that stage that you had a "tenant".'

'I was going to,' she had to admit. 'As soon as you came downstairs I was going to take great delight in throwing you out. Only by the time I saw you again I had found a note from Mrs Lloyd—she's the lady who used to work for my grandfather. The note was meant for Johnny, apologising that she wasn't able to look after his guest. I was still ready to throw you out, though,' she owned. 'Only before I had the chance you said something about Johnny being your new and soon to be short-lived assistant, and…'

'And?' Leon prompted when she hesitated.

'Well, Johnny loved that job so much. And—and it looked as if you were about to sack him. I couldn't…' Her voice faded. 'I couldn't let you. I couldn't just walk away and let you do that.'

'You couldn't?'

She shook her head. 'Johnny so wanted that job, and I knew just how desperate he would be to keep it.'

'So desperate that he told me this morning that he would be staying in Australia and intended writing to me with his resignation?'

'Hasn't he done that yet?' she exclaimed, though didn't know why she was surprised. It was so typically Johnny in 'airy-fairy-other-priorities' mode.

'You knew he was going to resign?' Leon picked up.

There seemed little point in denying anything now. 'He rang on Friday, wanting to speak with you to—'

'Last Friday?' Leon took up—as, had she been thinking at all clearly she would have realised that he would. 'You never thought to give me the message?'

She did not care too much to be taken to task. 'Johnny said he would write to you. I—er—believed he meant to do it that day.'

'You didn't tell him that I was still there—at Aldwyn House?'

'He was all sort of excited about getting married.'

'So he didn't know you'd been doing a housekeeping stint for me?' Varnie shook her head, and Leon gave her a frustrated kind of look. 'What goes on, Varnie?' he wanted to know. 'You obviously care very much for Metcalfe. To the extent you'd stay on cooking and cleaning for me—in property *you own*—just to ensure he keeps a job he wanted so badly he's given it up without thinking twice. You—'

'Johnny *did* love that job with you.' She defended her brother. Though suddenly saw that was irrelevant, and could only fall back on, 'Protecting Johnny has become something of a habit, I suppose,' she said lamely.

'Protecting him? Why would he need protecting?' Leon demanded, as she had known, as sharp as a tack.

'I don't know!' She was getting exasperated. 'Johnny's different. He has trouble settling down to things. He's clever,' she defended, 'but—but...' Helplessly, she gave it up. 'I love him,' she said simply—and saw what she had said seemed to have shaken Leon rigid.

'You *love* him?' he demanded tautly.

Varnie did not like his tone. 'Why wouldn't I?' she retorted, and, suddenly realising that the need for pretence and evasions was completely gone, she took a breath and stated, 'He's—my brother.'

Leon stared at her as though he could not believe his hearing. 'Metcalfe's your *brother*?' He seemed totally stunned for several seconds, as if such a relationship had never occurred to him.

Guilt swamped her. 'I'm sorry,' she apologised faintly.

But Leon was not long in sifting through what she had just told him. 'His name's Metcalfe; yours in Sutton. Heavens above!' he exclaimed, and actually seemed to lose some of his colour. 'Don't tell me now that you're married! That Sutton's your married name?'

'Of course it isn't! I'm not married!' she exclaimed abruptly, but calmed down to explain, 'If you want me to be more precise, Johnny is my stepbrother. His father married my mother when I was two. But Johnny has always been my brother.'

Leon stared at her incredulously for more stunned seconds. 'My stars, Varnie Sutton!' he grunted, shaking his head. But was soon back to his demanding best. 'Is that the truth?' he insisted.

'It is,' she confirmed, and actually found a smile as she

apologetically told him, 'I'm sorry if it hurts your pride, but…'

'There's more at stake here than my pride!' he retorted forthrightly.

And while Varnie wasn't sure what, if anything, to make of that statement, she felt she could safely confess, 'It's a relief not to have to lie to you any more. I don't usually tell lies,' she admitted. And, because she only ever wanted to be friends with him, 'Are you going to forgive me?'

'Why should I?' he asked aggressively.

'Why shouldn't you?' she replied, and with an impish smile, not wanting him cross with her, 'You know you like me.'

'Like you?' he questioned harshly, and very near made her collapse when, in the same harsh tone, he rapped, 'Dammit woman. I *love* you!'

Varnie did not know which one of them was the more surprised. 'You—don't!' she gasped.

'I didn't mean to tell you like that!' he retorted curtly. 'You've got me so wound up I don't know what I'm saying.'

She'd got *him* wound up—it was her turn to be stunned. 'I—have?' she asked, with what voice she could find.

'You have!' he answered tersely.

'Do you?' she asked tentatively, nervously.

'Do I what?'

She swallowed. 'Love me?'

'What the hell do you think I'm doing here now if it's not because loving you is driving me demented?' he barked.

She still did not believe it, yet felt she knew enough of Leon to know that he would not declare that he loved her if love her he did not. 'I think that's the nicest thing you've ever said to me,' she said softly.

And at her words, her softly given response to his admission of his love for her, Leon stared long and hard at her. And then he was demanding, 'Then would you very much mind telling me what the devil you're doing over there on that sofa, and what I'm doing over here on this one?'

He did not wait for her answer, but was on his feet. Varnie, her heart thundering away against her ribs, was on her feet too by the time he reached her. She was totally unresisting when tenderly he took her in his arms. For long, long moments, as if neither was quite believing that this was happening, they just stood and looked at each other. Then, gently, he kissed her.

'And—how do you feel about me?' Leon asked, his harsh manner completely gone as he pulled back to look into her sea-green eyes.

'I think you know,' she murmured shyly.

'My powers of deduction seem to have deserted me where you're concerned,' he answered, with an encouraging smile at her shyness. 'I have just now been able to take heart from the fact that when you've known since last Friday that you could have thrown me out without it being detrimental to Metcalfe, you did not. You, in actual fact, neither threw me out nor departed yourself. Instead you stayed—with me.'

Her mouth fell open a fraction. 'You're much too sharp!' she protested. 'Much too quick at seeing into matters.'

'Seeing into matters is what I do.' He grinned, but went on with a warm, teasing look, 'What I can't see is why— since last Friday—you would stay on with me—let alone not turf me out—if you did not care a little something for me?'

'I wanted to stay with you,' she confessed. 'I thought that if you were staying another two weeks, perhaps I could stay those two weeks with you too.'

'Little darling,' he said softly, and, because he had to, he kissed her.

'Oh!' she sighed as their kiss broke.

His kissed her again. And with his arms still about her he sat down with her on the sofa and questioned tenderly,

'Last night, when you came to my room, everything got too much for you, didn't it? That was why you bolted. Bolted without stopping to pack.'

'You checked? You went to my room and saw my belongings were still there?'

'I checked,' he confirmed. 'And thought—feared—that for all you hadn't shown the smallest sign of being terrified, to bolt without your possessions must mean that I'd come on much too strong and—'

'Not a bit of it!' she butted in quickly, and wanted only to be truthful from now on. 'You were so gentle, so tender with me, so—well—pretty wonderful, actually,' she confessed, blushing slightly. But if she were going to be truthful, making a full confession... 'I wanted our lovem... I wanted to stay. Only...' She hesitated as shyness unexpectedly blocked her path.

'Only?' Leon prompted softly.

Varnie swallowed down her shyness and opened up to answer, 'I wanted to stay with you from the love I have for you—' She broke off when his arm about her shoulders tightened. Leon looked as if he wanted to kiss her for her confession that she had love for him. But he held back, and she continued, 'I wanted to tell you of my feelings for you, only it suddenly hit me that as far as you were concerned love had no part in what we were doing.'

'Sweet love,' Leon breathed, and held her close up against him for ageless, marvellous moments. Then, gently, he kissed her. 'Oh, my darling, love had everything to do with it. I have known I was in love with you, that I loved you with everything that's in me, since that night you had a puncture on the way back from here.'

She looked at him, her heart thundering away inside of her, and wanted to sit there, just looking and looking at him. He, Leon Beaumont, loved her! Loved her—Varnie Sutton! 'That was—Thursday,' she documented, with what thinking power she could find.

'It was Thursday,' he agreed, smiling his love for her. 'Though I must have been heading in the "love" direction before then.' He kissed her again as if he could not help it, and added, 'There were many indications before last Thursday. I, in my superior wisdom, decided to ignore them.'

'What signs?' she had to know. Would her heart ever stop beating its present thundering beat?

'I love you,' he said, and her heart thundered some more.

'I can't believe it,' she whispered blissfully. 'But do go on.'

He kissed her, because it was the way he felt, and obliged. 'Signs such as missing you when you were out. Assuring myself that of course I wasn't missing you—what nonsense. And when I went out without you having to make myself stay out—I wasn't going to give in to this ridiculous urge to rush back to you.'

'Oh,' she sighed. 'And?'

'You're a devil for punishment,' Leon said with a smile, and held her close again, as if he loved how it felt to have her this close in his arms. 'And,' he indulged her, 'making myself believe it was my creature comforts I minded about when one day you asked if I'd be put out if you left.'

'You blackmailed me into staying.'

He grinned. 'Not my usual tactic—the writing must have been on the wall even then.'

She grinned back and, her heart full, wanted to tell him that she loved him. Realising then that she could, shyly she told him, 'I love you so very much.' And was not thinking at all for all of five minutes as Leon gathered her to him and they kissed, and held, and, their kisses growing warmer and warmer, Varnie had no thought to call a halt.

It was Leon who seemed to come to first. To come to an awareness that they were in her home, her parents' home, and that for all he knew her parents might return at any moment.

'See what happens when you say things like that to me?' he asked ruefully.

'So,' she said, striving hard to think what they had been talking about, 'you—um—started seeing me as something other than a housekeeper you were obliged to put up with?'

'That I did,' he confirmed, and took up, 'I started sleeping badly.'

'I've been there,' she said with a laugh—and was kissed for her trouble.

'Then I began to find that I liked having you around.'

'I shall start to purr any time now,' Varnie threatened.

'You were lippy, gave no quarter, but—I realised—I liked you.'

'You did?' she fished. 'Even though I was lippy?'

'Lippy—and stimulating. I even relished our verbal spats.' She grinned deliciously at him, and he had to kiss her once more before admitting, 'Had I been paying any heed, I should have picked up the warning signals. I was only ever meaning to stay away from London for a few days, a week at the most, then I discovered that I actually did not want to go back yet.'

'Oh!' she sighed blissfully, and could not resist asking, 'Did—I—er—have anything to do with that?'

He stared at her, his eyes drinking in her face. 'Lippy—and beautiful,' he said softly, and went on to frankly confirm, 'I felt certain, after the furious and despicable way I behaved after Neville King had left that Sunday, that one or other of us should leave too. Yet I didn't want to be the one to go—and I knew then that I didn't want you to go either.'

'Leon.' She murmured his name, purely from the joy and freedom to be able to do so, and they kissed, and held, and minutes passed, and she had no coherent thoughts. 'And then...?' she sighed, not totally sure what she must be asking.

She didn't think Leon knew much about what they had

been speaking of either, for all he had a stab at it. 'And then, with you looking sensational, we had dinner at Ruthin Castle, and you were giving me palpitations by kissing me.'

Varnie stared at him. 'You...I was giving you palpitations!'

'You were being unfair. I was doing my best to show you you could trust me—and you go and do a thing like that.'

'I was showing *you* that I trusted you. You'd trusted me with some confidences... Palpitations?'

He gave her a crooked smile. 'You kissed me, Varnie Sutton, and I had the hardest work in the world to not take you into my arms.' He planted a loving kiss to the tip of her dainty nose and confessed, 'I knew for sure that night that something was happening to me.'

'Oh!' she sighed, and confessed, 'I fell a little in love with you that night.'

'You darling,' he breathed. But took her to task to enquire, 'So why, when I gave in to the feeling of wanting to spend more time with you, did you refuse to eat with me, and annoy me by refusing to spend the next day with me when I went into town?

'Oh!' she exclaimed in surprise.

'It didn't matter,' he assured her. 'I spent the whole day trying to tell myself I wasn't bothered. Huh! But I had to admit to myself last Thursday, when you came to my room to tell me you had to go to your parents, that you were very special to me, Varnie mine.'

'Really?' she asked softly.

'I spent most of the afternoon watching out of the window for you coming back.'

'You...!'

'Crazy,' he admitted. 'The logical side of my brain knew full well not to expect you back yet. But love and logic don't seem to make very good bedfellows.'

'You—um—knew you loved me then?'

He shook his head. 'It was there, but I hadn't accepted

what had happened to me until, driving as fast as I dared in those appalling conditions, the sooner to get to you that night, I caught this bedraggled scrap of humanity in my headlights. And as my heart swelled with emotion I just knew that I was in love with you and that I wanted to keep you safe.'

Varnie couldn't get over what he had just said. She must have been looking the very worst she could possibly look— soaked, and with her hair and clothes plastered to her— bedraggled, as he'd said—yet that was when Leon had known that he loved her! 'You wrapped me in a blanket— and I wanted to tell you that I loved you,' she confessed.

'Sweetheart,' he breathed, and they kissed again, then he drew back and, looking into her melting sea-green eyes, asked, 'If I'm very good, shall I be permitted to come to Australia with you?'

'You want to come to Australia with us?' she gasped.

'Last Thursday, as I waited for you to come back, was a day that went on for ever,' he answered. 'If it's all the same to you, I'd prefer not to have to spend another day without you.'

Varnie just looked at him speechlessly. He loved her that much? 'Of course you're permitted.' She beamed. Though, even then protective of her brother, 'Don't think badly of Johnny. He—'

'Is he as protective of you as you are of him?' Leon butted in.

And she smiled again. 'Always has been,' she replied. 'I remember one time, he could have been no more than eight years old, I'd been crying in the middle of the night over a stray cat that had got run over. Johnny heard me and came and got into my bed and cuddled me better. I believe his father later came and carried a sleeping Johnny back to his own bed.'

Leon shook his head ruefully. 'That's the second reason I have to be grateful to John Metcalfe,' he stated.

'And the first?'

'There was I, so fed up with women—one way and another they'd been giving me a load of hassle of late—when, regardless of any sex discrimination act, I decided I wasn't going to put myself at risk of being compromised. I wasn't going to have a female assistant going around the country and overseas with me...'

'This would be when you wanted an additional assistant?'

'That was when.'

'You chose Johnny.'

'He was the only male to apply,' Leon answered. 'And up to a point he did a good job.'

'He fell down on the job when he—er—found you Aldwyn House.'

'That's what I thought—but only to start with. I'd had my fill of scheming women, and needed some space, some solitude. Metcalfe—er—John said he knew the very place, yet before I've got my eyes open on my first morning there a totally stark naked woman is in my room, accosting me.'

'Accosting!' Varnie choked. And Leon laughed a wonderful laugh.

'So I have to thank him.'

'Thank him?' she queried adoringly.

'Had he not known of this place of solitude I should never have met his beautiful and delightful sister.'

'Oh, Leon.'

'My lovely Varnie,' he said softly, and kissed her. Then he pulled back. 'My heart is so full of you I thought I'd die when I discovered your note this morning and realised I didn't have any idea of your address.'

'You found me,' she whispered.

'And I'm going to keep you,' he promised solemnly. And when, with love in her eyes, Varnie looked at him, he kissed her tenderly, and after some moments reminded her, 'You said you did hotel work. Was that another one of your howlers?'

'I shall never lie to you again,' she promised, and went on to reveal, 'Until fairly recently my parents owned a hotel. I worked for them.'

Leon took that on board, then again reminded her, 'You said you were looking for other work.'

'Did I?'

'You've told so many you can't remember?'

She had to laugh. 'I had thought of getting myself a career,' she told him truthfully.

Leon thought that over for a moment, and then asked, 'Do you think you could fit your career in with a—vocation—I have for you?'

Vocation? What vocation could that be? 'You—want me to work for you?' she guessed. And oddly, watching him, she thought that he seemed strangely nervous suddenly. And that *was* odd. She had never seen Leon nervous!

But his grey eyes were warm on her puzzled sensitive green eyes when, tenderly, he told her, 'I love you so very much, Varnie. Come to me, my darling,' he urged. And, shaking her to her very foundations, 'Come to me,' he breathed, 'and be my wife?'

She stared at him, speechless. Her mouth fell a little way open. 'F-for real, you mean?' she managed hesitantly.

'Most definitely for real,' he answered, his expression never more serious. 'Please say yes, that you'll marry me?'

As he waited for his answer she saw that he seemed to be under some degree of stress. But he did not have to wait very long, because her answer did not require any thinking about.

'Oh, Leon,' she cried. 'I'd love to marry you—if you're sure!'

'My darling!' he exclaimed joyously, her acceptance of his proposal all he wanted to hear. Leon drew her closer to his heart. 'I've never been more sure of anything in my life,' he murmured. 'Sweet love, I want you with me always.'

HIS HEIRESS WIFE by **Margaret Way** *(The Australians)*

Olivia Linfield was the beautiful heiress; Jason Corey was the bad-boy made good. It should have been the wedding of the decade – except it never took place. Seven years later Olivia returns to discover Jason installed as estate manager. Will he persuade Olivia how much he still wants her, and always has...?

THE HUSBAND SWEEPSTAKE by **Leigh Michaels**
(What Women Want!)

Erika Forrester has fought hard to get where she is, and is used to living her life free from the stresses of relationships. But now she needs help – she needs a husband, fast! There's only one candidate she'll consider – Amos Abernathy, the best husband Manhattan has to offer!

HER SECRET, HIS SON by **Barbara Hannay**

When Mary Cameron left Australia she was carrying a secret – a secret she's kept to herself for years. But now Tom Pirelli is back, and she's forced to confront the choices she made. It's Mary's chance to tell Tom the real reason she left him – and that he's the father of her child...

MARRIAGE MAKE-OVER by **Ally Blake**
(To Have and To Hold)

Kelly loves every minute of being single – she even writes a column about it! But she harbours a secret she can never tell her readers: she's married! She hasn't seen her husband in five years, but now her famed column has brought Simon hotfooting it back to Melbourne...

On sale 3rd September 2004

MILLS & BOON®

Volume 3
on sale from
3rd September
2004

Lynne
Graham

International Playboys

*The Desert
Bride*

FREE

4 BOOKS AND A SURPRISE GIFT!

We would like to take this opportunity to thank you for reading this Mills & Boon® book by offering you the chance to take FOUR more specially selected titles from the Tender Romance™ series absolutely FREE! We're also making this offer to introduce you to the benefits of the Reader Service™—

- ★ **FREE home delivery**
- ★ **FREE gifts and competitions**
- ★ **FREE monthly Newsletter**
- ★ **Books available before they're in the shops**
- ★ **Exclusive Reader Service offers**

Accepting these FREE books and gift places you under no obligation to buy; you may cancel at any time, even after receiving your free shipment. Simply complete your details below and return the entire page to the address below. You don't even need a stamp!

YES! Please send me 4 free Tender Romance books and a surprise gift. I understand that unless you hear from me, I will receive 6 superb new titles every month for just £2.69 each, postage and packing free. I am under no obligation to purchase any books and may cancel my subscription at any time. The free books and gift will be mine to keep in any case.

N4ZEE

Ms/Mrs/Miss/Mr...Initials ....
                                                                      BLOCK CAPITALS PLEASE

Surname ....

Address ....

....

....Postcode ....

Send this whole page to:
The Reader Service, FREEPOST CN81, Croydon, CR9 3WZ